ONE HUNDRED CHANCES

AN ASPEN COVE SMALL TOWN ROMANCE

KELLY COLLINS

BOOK NOOK PRESS

CHAPTER ONE

Sara Arden had done a lot of things wrong in her life, but having Reese wasn't one of them. Keeping her from her father might have been. In her defense, she didn't have a choice. She learned a long time ago it wasn't wise to dwell on what was and what could have been. The past was something that happened to her, but the future was in her control. Or that was what she believed until that moment.

As she stared into Lloyd Dawson's eyes, a thousand emotions came back, but surprise was the most pronounced. As for control, she lost it the minute his lips turned into a smile and her heart danced in her chest like it belonged to the sixteen-year-old girl who'd fallen in love with him all those years ago.

"Sara? Is that you?" he asked as he walked into the diner where she was having lunch with her daughter and Brandon. His eyes went from her to Reese. It was hard to hide the resemblance, as they both had reddish-brown hair and the same-colored eyes. Everything about their faces was identical, from the lines of their noses to the dimples on their chins. There was no concealing Reese was his, and when his eyes hardened into chips of ice and his expression turned to stone, she realized he knew as well.

She looked at her daughter. "Oh, shit." Her heart took off like a greyhound chasing a rabbit. Anxiety ripped through her system like a cyclone. The last time she got this nervous was that summer day, decades ago, when she held the pregnancy test in her hand and told her parents. In hindsight, maybe she should have told Lloyd first, because the second the truth was out, she was whisked away, and her life was no longer hers.

Lloyd pointed to a different booth at the far end of the diner. "I think we need to talk." His voice was stern. But then he turned to Reese, tipping his head and laying on the charm. "Hello, darlin', I'm Lloyd, but you might already know that."

Sara rolled her eyes, but Reese smiled brightly.

"Nice to meet you, Lloyd. I'm Reese, and this is my boyfriend, Brandon."

Lloyd narrowed his eyes. "Son, I believe you and I will also have a talk soon."

Brandon chuckled. "Yes, sir. I'm sure we will. It's nice to meet you."

He glared at Sara, then nodded toward the empty booth. "By the looks of it, you're about thirty-odd years behind schedule, so how about we have that chat now?" He posed it as a question, but he wasn't asking.

Sara frowned. She wasn't used to being pushed around by anyone. It had taken her decades to find herself, and she wasn't letting any man, even one as handsome as Lloyd Dawson, take her power away. "Actually, I'm kind of busy right now. I'm enjoying lunch with my daughter." She put emphasis on the word "my." Sara had raised Reese, and she didn't want Lloyd to come in here and smooth-talk his way into Reese's heart. He may have been the donor who helped bring Reese to life, but Sara was the doer. "If you want to talk to me, then I suggest you get on my calendar. I'll be here a few days."

Lloyd stepped back as if she'd slapped him. She imagined he wasn't a man used to taking orders from anyone, but since her parents passed, neither was she.

He stared at her, and she swore his face turned to stone. He didn't say a single word before he turned and stomped away to where the deputy sheriff sat with a beautiful woman.

"So, that's my daddy, huh?"

"That big oaf is not your daddy. You don't have a daddy. He was …" She let out a gurgling growl. "He's changed."

Reese doctored the coffee Maisey had poured and smiled. She was enjoying the discomfort this was causing. "I imagine you're not the same as you were when you were sixteen, either," she said. "Back then, you were probably fun."

"Hey." She pointed a slim finger at Reese. "I'm still fun."

"You are not fun. The only time you're marginally bearable is when you're drunk." She gasped. "Oh, my God. Were you two drunk when you got knocked up?"

Sara leaned in and whispered, "Reese Owen Arden, you keep your voice down. If you want to mar your reputation and talk about yourself, that's fine, but you will not tarnish mine by shouting to the town that I was getting jiggy under the deck with a Dawson."

"Jiggy? Geez, Mom. You'd make every nineties sitcom proud. I'd say your reputation sailed at sixteen."

"You have no idea what it was like to be me."

"No, but I know what it was like to be me, and it wasn't fun." Reese frowned. "Why did you lie to me?"

"I didn't lie to you. I withheld some of the truth."

"You don't get to twist the story. I asked you who my father was, and you told me the stork?"

"Things aren't always rainbows and unicorns. Back then, my life was complicated." She pinched the bridge of her nose. "What started out as a fib turned into something colossal."

Reese nearly choked on her coffee. "Like a six-pound, twelve-ounce baby girl fib? How was that winter in Sheboygan, Wisconsin?"

"What are you talking about?"

Reese shook her head. "Grandma. I figured she sent you away to a convent, hidden in some winter hell up north until you delivered."

Maisey dropped off three plates of burgers and fries, but they weren't regular burgers. They were open-faced chiliburgers with cheese fries. The kind that put an extra five pounds of ass on a backend from a single meal.

"Do you even remember your grandmother?"

Reese shrugged. "I remember the dresses. Oh, how I hated those dresses." She tapped her chin. "You know what? That was probably the childhood trauma that made me stutter. It wasn't me drowning in the lake. It was the dresses and the pin curls she insisted I wear to get my hair under control." She ran her hands through her curly hair. "I bet my hair was like yours—straight as a ruler. But those weekends you made me spend at her house where she dressed me like an American Girl doll and twisted my hair in pin curls that stayed tucked tightly to my head. My poor hair just gave up and gave in."

Brandon kissed her cheek. "I love your curls. I wouldn't change a thing about you."

Sara snorted. "Just wait until you've spent months listening to her smart mouth." She picked up a chili-coated fry and pointed it at him. "I'm telling you, I'm not taking her back." She popped the fry into her mouth, chewed, and swallowed. "You wanted her and now you have to keep her." A chill passed down her spine, and she resisted the urge to turn around. "Is he shooting icy daggers at me?" She could feel Lloyd's cold stare. It was like being stabbed by a thousand frozen icicles, and it wasn't even winter.

"He's looking this way. Maybe he's interested." Reese laughed. "Can you imagine? After all these years, my parents meet again and fall in love." She pulled a pen from her bag and scribbled on a napkin. "This is good. I need to write it down."

"He's a married man," Sara said, while she swirled another french fry through the chili. As recent events transpired, it was more important than ever for her to go back to Oklahoma, and fast. When Lloyd walked up to her, all those old butterflies swirled inside her stomach. That man had turned her life upside down once, and she wasn't going to let him do it again. What was she thinking? She may have been a silly sixteen-year-old who got pregnant, but she drew a hard line with married men. Especially those with children. He no doubt had several more flowers to fill that vase of his.

"No, he's not married." Brandon cut into his burger and held a bite to his lips. "He's a widower," he said, before plopping it into his mouth.

Reese looked at him. "How do you know?"

He swallowed and chuckled. "You're not the only one who listens. Besides, he was about to murder two of the town's firemen the day they dug up the beach."

"Dug up the beach," Sara said. "Who dug up the beach? What were they looking for?"

Brandon and Reese smiled. "Me?" Reese said. "In the end, they were looking for me. Brandon had a map of sorts, and there was an X on it. It said something like everything you're looking for is here. The town came out to help him find the treasure."

Sara wasn't sure she wanted to know. "Another one of your book fantasies?"

Her daughter tucked her head into Brandon's shoulder. It was odd to watch Reese with a man, and while she was happy for her, a tinge of jealousy swept through her. There was a lot to be analyzed about their mother-daughter relationship and codependence. She wouldn't take the blame for it all. All you had to do was look at Reese and see she'd released her mother and become dependent on Brandon.

She couldn't fault her. Some people were like that, and Reese hadn't been independent since the drowning when she was five. That was where Sara was at fault. The guilt of not being there was over-whelming and there wasn't a day, even now, when she didn't think about it. She'd let a man distract her and almost lost her daughter.

That day, she'd left Reese with Brandy Bennett because she'd seen Lloyd on the beach a few houses down, and she was finally going to come clean. That decision to leave those two together changed everything.

She glanced over her shoulder and caught Lloyd staring at her. It wasn't the icy look she expected—the one where she'd freeze solid and disintegrate into shards once touched—but one of curiosity. She was like one of those stick bugs you hear about but only see every once in a while—an oddity.

"You really should talk to him, Mom."

Sara sighed. "I know, but it's been decades. What do I say?"

"Seems to me like you'd have a lot to discuss." Reese quirked a brow and cocked her head.

"We do, but he'll want to know why, and..."

Reese thinned her lips. "Mother, I think you owe us both an explanation."

She nodded. "I do, but I wanted to tell you first."

"Okay. I'm ready."

Sara took a deep breath. Sooner was better than later because she wasn't planning on staying in Aspen Cove any longer than she had to. "It's not all that complicated when you understand the family dynamics. In our circle, all you have to know is we are Ardens."

"What does that mean?"

Her mother gave her a sad smile. "You were born Reese Owen Arden, daughter of Catherine and Frank Arden, Sr."

Reese's jaw dropped. "What?"

"You weren't too far off when you said I was sent to Sheboygan. Mom and I went abroad to France, and you were born there. When we came back, I had a sister, and you had a nanny while I finished school."

"But you're my mother."

She nodded. "I know that, and you know that, and everyone else knows it, but polite society would never say anything."

"Since I've never seen my birth certificate, given that I've never had a traditional job and didn't need it, and you provided documentation when I got my driver's license, I'll assume I was listed as yours and Uncle Frank's sibling?"

"You were."

Reese laughed. "That makes me a third owner of the beach house."

"Don't push your luck, kiddo. You weren't put in the will."

Reese snapped her fingers. "I knew they never liked me."

"Not true. They adored you. They tolerated me, but they were a stickler for tradition and had a specific type of man they deemed suitable. That man wasn't Lloyd." Sara closed her eyes and remembered the fights she had with her mother about the handsome cowboy. "He was from the wrong side of the tracks, according to them."

Reese frowned. "Do you realize you tried to run Brandon away in the same manner?"

Sara reached across the table and set her hand on Brandon's. That day, among many others, was not a proud moment. "I think we all turn into our mothers from time to time. In my defense, all I can say is no man will ever be good enough for my daughter, and it has nothing to do with you, Brandon. You could be the best man in the world, and you would still fall short of my expectations because, contrary to popular belief, I love this kid ... kid being a relative term to my age. She's all I have, and I want what's best for her."

He smiled. "I will do my best to make her happy." Chuckling, he said, "Because if I don't, I've been told you know how to put big animals down."

Reese gasped. "Did you tell him that?"

Sara sat up and grinned. "I did, and I do, and I'll stand by that statement. I will not be kind to you if you hurt my daughter." She looked at her barely touched plate and reached into her bag to pull out a twenty. "Thanks for letting me dine with you. I love you, Reese. I'm sorry our lives have been so complex, but life can be tricky. Let's work on simplifying things, okay?"

"You haven't eaten much," Reese said.

"I've lost my appetite."

Reese glanced toward Lloyd's table. "I'd like to talk to my father if you're okay with that."

"I don't want to hold you back. I've been in your way long enough." She rose and slung her bag over her shoulder.

Reese reached for her hand. "Mom, that's not true. I think you've been in your own way."

Sara gave her hand a squeeze and waited until Lloyd was talking to the girl sitting next to him before she made her escape. Even though she owed him an explanation, she wasn't ready to face him now. She had one goal when coming to Aspen Cove, and that was to convince her daughter to come home. But seeing Reese happy and in love, Sara could return to Oklahoma feeling confident her daughter would be okay.

Reese could forge a relationship with her father if she wanted, but Sara didn't have to be a part of that. Reese had the basic details of what happened, and as a storyteller, she could weave a good tale for Lloyd. If Sara hurried, she could get to the house, pack, and get out of Aspen Cove without a confrontation.

She bolted from the diner and was almost to her car when a hand touched her elbow. When she looked up, those sexy Dawson eyes pinned her in place. "Where do you think you're going?"

CHAPTER TWO

Lloyd stood on Main Street, staring at Sara. He hadn't seen her in decades, but as soon as he walked into the diner, he recognized her straight out. A man never forgot his first love. She was part of who he was and who he'd become. Sara was the first girl to capture his heart and the first to shatter it. He wasn't letting her slip away again without a conversation.

"Let go of me." She tugged herself free from his grip.

"I did that years ago and see where it got me? Now I'm not letting you go until you tell the truth." He pointed toward the diner. "Reese is mine, isn't she?"

Sara stood with her back as stiff and straight as a ruler. "No, she's mine." She tried to get bigger by raising onto her tiptoes, but her five-foot-five frame wouldn't intimidate a man like him. "Now let me go." She looked like a caged animal, and the one thing Lloyd knew about trapped animals was once they were cornered, they were unpredictable. He dropped his grip on her and stepped back as a crack of thunder shook the skies. Seconds later, they opened up to a torrential downpour.

"Let's go back inside." He took the edge of his flannel and held it over her head to protect her from the elements. What started as large drops of rain quickly turned into tiny pebbles of hail, then pea-size, then dimes. They pelted him in the face and head and body. Little sharp stings pricked at his skin. "Sara, I'm taking a beating here. Let's go inside and talk like adults."

She held her arms above her head for protection and moved forward as if she were going to join him, so he dashed to the diner door, only to realize she'd stopped a few feet back. When he whipped around, she was climbing into her car.

"Sara," he yelled. "It's not safe to drive." The road turned white as the unexpected summer hailstorm rained down.

She stared at him for a second before she backed her car out of the parking spot and took off down the street, fishtailing on the slick pavement. He walked back into the diner with nothing to show but drenched clothing and prickly red dots where he'd been clipped by the larger hailstones.

Poppy and Mark stared at him from the booth, and he held up a finger to tell them he'd be there in a second, then turned toward Reese and Brandon. "I apologize for my abrupt greeting. I'm a man of few words and fewer still when I looked at you." He examined Reese's features. She was the doppelgänger of his mother, who he resembled the most. "You look exactly like your grandmother."

Reese shook her head. "I don't think so. She was blonde and always had a constipated expression."

He laughed. "Not Catherine. I met her once, and I remember that look. I'm referring to my mother, Iris." He glanced at his daughter Poppy, whose eyes were full of questions. "I'd like to talk more, but in private, without the entire town present. You may not know about small towns, but the diner is like a megaphone, and what happens here will be heard worldwide."

"I understand." Reese nodded. "Before you go, I want to point out that neither of us has acknowledged that you're my father."

"It would seem I am, and we have a lot of catching up to do." He loved how her eyes were so expressive. It was like she didn't need to speak, and he'd know what she was thinking. "I bet you have a lot of questions." He glanced around the diner, which held the usual cast of characters from Doc to the Williams, and some of the fire crew. "How long have you known?" He imagined she had come here looking for him. He remembered her from the beach that day. Everyone was looking for a treasure but he didn't put it all together until now. "If I wasn't so focused on Daisy and Violet's flirtatious behavior, I may have put the pieces together."

"I didn't know then, and I wasn't sure until a male version of myself walked inside the diner. I've never had a father. My mom told me the stork had delivered me."

Lloyd laughed. "And you believed her?"

"Until I was six. Then I learned storks were birds, and they didn't deliver babies."

"You've always had a father. We just didn't know." He looked over his shoulder at Poppy. "I have some explaining to do with my kids. How can I get in touch with you?"

She reached inside her bag and pulled out her business card. He stared at the words: romance ghostwriter.

"You're even more like your grandma than I imagined. She loved romance books." He tucked the card into his back pocket. "They call them bodice rippers, right? My wife used to read them too."

Reese smiled at him. "Yes. Read a romance novel if you ever want to know what a woman wants."

"I'll keep that in mind if I'm ever in the market for a woman." A loud crack of thunder dimmed the lights, and the thunk of bigger hail hit the roof. He looked out the window at ice chunks the size of golf balls coming down. "Better call your insurance carrier. There's going to be a lot of damage." He turned to walk away, but stopped. "Your mother took off like a hare being chased by a fox. I hope she made it home okay." By now, everyone in the diner was crowded around the door and windows, looking at the natural disaster unfolding. Hailstorms were common in the summer, but golf-ball-sized hail was not.

He walked over to Poppy and took a seat. "Looks like we're in for a rough summer."

She glanced outside and then back at him. "You're not talking about the weather, are you? Is there something I need to know about that girl over there?"

He nodded. "Lots, but I don't know much either."

Poppy cocked her head. "Let's start with why she looks exactly like you?"

Lloyd watched the hail come down outside and batter the cars parked on Main Street. He'd been pummeled too, only his was an emotional beating. The dents and broken glass could be fixed, but would he recover from what he found out? He had a daughter. Reese was about thirty-two if he did the calculations correctly in his head. "That is your older sister, Reese."

Poppy stared at him for an eternity before she said, "Obviously, this was before Mom. Did you know?"

He shook his head. "Not until I walked inside the diner. Reese's mother, Sara, was my first love."

"Wow. Is that the woman you chased after when she ran from the diner?"

"Yes."

"Holy mackerel. It's hard to imagine you being in love with anyone other than Mom."

"Your mom was my life."

Poppy looked past him to Reese. "Not your whole life. I bet Sara was a stunner back then because she's still beautiful now."

He thought so too, but he'd keep that to himself. "I didn't notice. Once I met your mother, I never looked back." He met Carol after Sara left that summer. He was heartbroken that he'd never heard from her again until she showed up five years later, but by then, he was married and Carol was pregnant with Poppy. "Don't tell your brother and sisters yet. I want a moment to digest it all first. Let's talk about it at Sunday dinner. Since everyone is home for the summer, it will be a good time to introduce Reese."

"Okay, Dad, but can I go over and say hello? I always wanted a big sister."

Poppy's husband, Mark, sat there the entire time with a perplexed look on his face.

"You got something to say?" Lloyd asked.

Mark chuckled. "No, sir." He laughed again. "Well, maybe. It looks like you're the proud father of a hundred and something pound bouncing baby girl."

Lloyd frowned. "Behave yourself, or I might need help mucking out the stalls." It was a shit job, literally, and one he used as a punishment when his kids misbehaved. Since Mark was Poppy's husband, he was close enough to being a son, and the rules applied to him, too.

Maisey rushed over. "Sorry about the wait. The roof is leaking, and Ben and I were putting pots down to catch the drips. What a nightmare." She pulled out her pen and pad. "What can I get you?"

Outside, a sliver of sun cut through the clouds, but the damage left in the storm's wake was extensive. Hellion was in the paddock and he hoped Basil had put him in the barn.

"Sorry, Maisey, my plan was to have a nice lunch with my daughter and son-in-law, but I need to check the damage at the ranch." He pulled a few twenties from his pocket. "I'd like to pick up my daughter's tab." Then he nodded to Reese and Brandon's table. "I'll get theirs as well."

Maisey raised a brow and smiled. "She looks just like you."

"Can you hold on to that secret for a few?"

Maisey laughed. "The only person who thinks it's a secret is you."

She was right. When he glanced around the diner again, all eyes were on them. He kissed Poppy on the cheek and shook Mark's hand. "See you two on Sunday." He rose from the booth and walked to Reese and Brandon's table. "How about dinner on Sunday? You can meet your brother and sisters."

Reese smiled brightly. "That sounds great. How many do I have?"

"Six. Poppy, Rose, Lily, Daisy, Violet, and Basil."

"You have a vase of flowers and a little spice on the side."

It was a good way to describe his family. "See you Sunday. I'll text you the directions." He turned and walked out of the diner. When he had gone inside, he was looking for a nice meal and some quality time with Poppy. What he got was a new daughter, a headache, and a lot of damage to his truck.

Taking a seat behind the wheel, he slowly headed toward home because the roads were still covered in hail. As he turned onto the highway leading to his ranch, two tire tracks disappeared off the edge of the embankment. A lump lodged in his throat as he pulled to the side of the road and exited. He knew what he'd find before he peeked over the edge. At the bottom of the ravine was Sara's car, upside down.

His heart raced as he half ran, half fell down the hillside. He came to the window, where Sara hung upside down, still strapped in her seat. A cut on her forehead dripped blood onto the ceiling of the sedan. "Sara?" The windshield was shattered, and the roof was caved in on the passenger's side, but her side was still intact. She sat there, staring straight ahead. "Sara, are you okay?"

In slow motion, she turned to face him. "Are you here to save me?"

He smiled. "I am."

"About time. If only you could have shown up thirty-two years ago when I needed you, I wouldn't be in this situation."

CHAPTER THREE

Her words were unfair, but it was the stress of the situation talking. She was trapped and couldn't escape, but it wasn't the time to have this conversation. She was injured, disoriented, and needed to be on solid ground to face Lloyd.

"If you're here to save me, you're going to have to do something. Stop staring and get me out of here. I've been waiting around for a lifetime to be rescued."

"I'm not sure I should move you." Lloyd got on his knees in the wet grass and took in the situation. "You could have life-threatening injuries."

"Just wait until I'm free, and I'll show you a life-threatening injury." She thrashed around trying to get out, but only ended up honking the horn and scaring herself.

Lloyd chuckled. "You need to stay put. You have a head injury, and that noise isn't going to help. Once Doc has looked at it, we'll get you out of here." He reached in and touched her shoulder. "I'll call for assistance." He pulled out his phone and dialed. A few seconds later, he said. "Hey, Mark, it's Lloyd. I need some help on the highway right as you leave town. Bring Doc and the boys." Lloyd leaned back and looked right and left at her car. "We'll need a tow too, so grab Bobby, and maybe Cade. See you in a few."

"Dammit, Lloyd, I've already assessed myself, and I'm fine. Cut me loose." She struggled against the seatbelt. "All the blood is rushing to my head, and I feel nauseous."

"You have a head injury, and that's why I don't want to move you."

Looking past her, he reached inside to grab something. When his hand came out with her purse, she groaned. "If you want money, I don't have any. I left it on the table for my meal. As a general rule, I don't use cash."

His hand came out with her package of Kleenex, and he pulled a few free and pressed them to her head. "In my experience, most women are better than Boy Scouts. They are always prepared. Especially women with children."

"I'd hardly call Reese a child."

He shook his head. "She's my child."

"Are you keeping me here as a form of torture because I didn't tell you?" She yanked at the seatbelt once more, and it painfully pulled at her neck.

"No, I'm keeping you here because you have a large gash at your hairline, and I don't know if moving you will make it worse."

She had no pain in her extremities. The only thing that hurt was her head, and that was throbbing before she drove off the side of the road. Why was it that everything painful had something to do with Lloyd Dawson? She shook her head because the thought was ridiculous. A sharp pain stabbed at her temple. Maybe she was being punished for keeping Reese from him.

"I told you, I already assessed myself and I'm fine."

"What makes you qualified to do that?"

"I'm a doctor."

His head snapped back. "Wow, I didn't know. What's your specialty?"

Lloyd mistook her for a physician for humans. Did she set him

straight or leave it be? The sirens in the background made the decision for her. She'd be free in minutes and wouldn't have to share
anything else with Lloyd. Wasn't sharing her daughter enough? He
wasn't entitled to any more than that. Out of the corner of her eye,
she watched several cars pull to the edge of the hill. "Finally.
Someone willing to lift a finger."

He stood and stepped back. "Don't forget it was these fingers that
called for help."

The first down the hill was a young firefighter. "Hello, ma'am.
My name is James, and I'm here to rescue you."

She let out a growl that could make a grown man run. "Standing
there doesn't do diddly. Cut me loose."

Lloyd held up a wad of Kleenex. "I applied direct pressure to the
wound, but as you can see, it's still bleeding."

She moved her hand to her head and pulled it back to see the
traces of blood. "It's because all the blood is rushing to my head. Get
me out of here." Another firefighter arrived with a first aid kit, and the
deputy sheriff came down the hill with Doc, who lowered himself
slowly to his knees.

"I'm getting too old for this." He took her pulse and checked her
for additional injuries. "Let's cut her down," he said. "Watch her
head."

Before she could blink, there was a firefighter on each side of her.
One had shimmied into the crushed side of her car to cut the belt
while the other supported her, so she didn't come down on her head.

Doc hovered over her as the firefighters put her on a board and
strapped her down, making sure her head was secure. "This town
could use an ambulance."

She tried to sit up but couldn't. "You don't have one? How am I
getting to the hospital?"

"Ain't got one of those, either." Doc looked at the firefighters.
"Load her up in the back of Lloyd's truck and take her to the clinic."

"Wait. What do you mean, load her up in the back of Lloyd's
truck?" she asked.

The two young firefighters lifted her. Doc groaned as he stood. "It's that or carry you all the way." He tapped the center of his bushy mustache. "I could call Copper Creek and have them send an ambulance, but that means you'll be here for another hour, and the sky doesn't look too good."

She glanced up to see dark swirling clouds. "Do you think it will hail again?"

Doc narrowed his eyes. "I'm not a weatherman. I'm a doctor. What's it going to be?"

A drop of water fell from the sky and landed right between her eyes. "Looks like I have little choice."

Lloyd moved closer into view. "You always have a choice." His lips pinched together so tightly they almost disappeared. "Are you capable of making the right one? As a doctor, I'd think you'd know what you're doing. This situation is going to quickly go from bad to worse in a few minutes."

Doc laughed. "Doctor? She's a veterinarian." He leaned over her. "Why don't you leave the humans to me and stick with the furry friends?"

Sara sucked in a breath. "I'll have you know I had to learn how to treat every species while you only have to doctor people."

Doc walked beside her as they carried her up the embankment. "Dogs don't talk back."

"No, but they bite."

Doc grumbled something about being ungrateful, and how he was missing *General Hospital*. "If you bite me, I'm sending you to Copper Creek in the back of Lloyd's truck."

She heard the tailgate open, and the sound of hail hit the road as they cleaned out the bed. When all was clear, they slid her onto the truck's bed. "Isn't someone riding with me?"

Doc looked up at the sky. "It's raining. Besides, it's a two-minute drive."

"But what if he crashes as I did?"

Lloyd chuckled. "Unlikely. I know how to drive."

She couldn't move, but she could talk. "Did you just call me a bad driver?"

He leaned over the side of the truck so she could see him. "I'm not the one who crashed. See you in a few minutes."

Everyone disappeared, and she was left strapped to a board in the back of Lloyd's truck. If ever she felt like one of the poor animals she treated, it was then. No one understood her apprehension, or they didn't care. She was piled into the back like a pig going to slaughter.

Another drop fell from the sky, then another, until she was sure she'd drown before they arrived. The truck stopped as the weather let loose, and the firefighters carried her through the pharmacy to an office.

They unstrapped her and transferred her to the exam table, where she quickly sat up and regretted it because of the ache in her head.

They waited for Doc to shuffle in. Right behind him was Lloyd. "Should I get our daughter?"

All eyes went to her. "Way to let out a secret." A sharp pain shot to her temple, and she lay down on the table.

"The only one keeping secrets is you." He turned to the others in attendance. "Not a word until I talk to my kids on Sunday."

The fireman named James looked at Lloyd. "Sir, I'd like to ask Lily on a date, but I wanted your permission first." Lloyd eyed the kid.

He was a kid to her because he had to be in his twenties and still had puppy brains. She'd read once that adult thinking didn't happen until a person was twenty-five. "No one asks permission anymore. Just ask the girl out."

Lloyd cleared his throat. "When it comes to my girls, everyone asks permission." He stared at James in silence for a few minutes. "When's your next day off?"

"Sunday, sir."

"How are you at mucking stalls?"

"I'm sorry. What?"

Sara laughed, even though it hurt. "Are you good at shoveling shit? You'll have to prove yourself it would seem."

James looked confused. "I have to shovel horse dung to date your daughter?"

"Yes, you do. Hard work shows the mettle of a man. I need to make sure you're willing to do the hard stuff before getting to the easy stuff." Realizing what he'd just said, he blurted, "My Lily is not easy."

"No, sir, she isn't."

Lloyd stepped toward James menacingly. "How would you know?"

Doc pointed to the door. "If you're not a doctor or a patient, get out."

Lloyd nodded. "I'll get Reese."

As soon as the others were gone, Doc turned to her. "Is Reese his child?"

"Yes, Reese is his," she sighed. "Are you going to stitch me up or what?"

Doc chuckled. "Or what covers it. It's a scrape with a couple of parts almost deep enough for a stitch, but I think we can clean it up, and it will heal on its own." He washed his hands, gloved up, and poured saline into a container. "Does she know?"

"She does now. I mean, look at her. She's Lloyd with boobs."

"For a small town, we sure have our share of drama." He pressed against her wound, and she winced.

"It's like a regular living hell here."

"It's all perspective. Maybe you should stay awhile. You might find that it's a slice of heaven."

"More like purgatory."

"You're right. You could use a few stitches." He pulled out a package and opened it, then went to a drawer to get a syringe and a bottle of lidocaine.

"Am I getting stitches because I said something bad about your town?" Doc was always possessive about Aspen Cove and its residents. He was back then, and she could see he was now. The old geezer probably couldn't help himself. It was in his blood as a relative of one of the founding families.

He jabbed her with the needle and numbed her up. "You need the stitches, but you also need perspective. All you have are the memories of a teenage girl who got caught in a bad way. If I were you, I'd be jaded too."

"I'm not jaded. I don't see what this town offers. There isn't even a bank."

Doc shook his head. "Not true. Both Maisey and I put one of those ATMs in our places. That's as good as any bank. You can make a deposit and take cash. If you need change, you can ask my Agatha."

She didn't have the energy to argue with him. "I guess it will do."

He handed her a mirror. "I'm going to leave it open to heal. It's right at your hairline so no one will notice." He gave the rest of her a thorough check. "You're lucky you didn't break anything." He pulled a small penlight from his pocket. "I don't think you have a concussion, but you know what to look for, being you're a doctor and all." Doc winked. "What do you tell your patients to look for?"

"Ha ha, you know I had more schooling than you."

Doc made a *tsk tsk* sound. "It all comes down to choices."

There was a commotion in the hall, and the door flew open. "Mom, are you okay?"

Sara hopped off the table and closed her eyes as the pain increased and then subsided. "I'm fine."

"Monitor her. Right now, she doesn't show signs of a concussion, but you never know. Her speech seems perfectly okay if her ranting is any sign."

Sara stomped her foot and regretted it immediately. "Ranting? I'll have you know—"

"Her pupils look right as rain, but that can change," Doc said, interrupting her.

"What about my car?"

"It's in Bobby Williams' hands now," Doc said.

"But I want to go back to Tulsa."

"Mom, it doesn't look like you're going anywhere but the beach house."

Lloyd stepped inside. "You don't get to escape that easily." He turned to Reese. "Bring her to dinner on Sunday." Then he walked out.

"I'm not mucking your stalls," Sara called out as he left.

CHAPTER FOUR

Lloyd sat on the porch with his shotgun by his side. When James showed up to muck stalls that morning, he wanted to make sure he set the tone. Nothing said, "Don't mess with my daughter," like a 20-gauge.

At five thirty, the sun was peeking over the mountains, and the birds chirped away as if doing a roll call to see if everyone made it through the night. This was Lloyd's favorite time of day. It was a time to reflect on what was to come and what had already passed. He used to enjoy a morning coffee on the porch with Carol before she got ill and passed away. Now he sat here alone because his girls milked every minute of sleep they could get, and his son Basil was no different. That boy would run out the door at a minute to six with a protein bar in one hand, a coffee in the other, and say he was ready.

Was he paying something back to the universe when he got five girls and one boy? As a rancher, he'd dreamed of many sons, but he had to admit his girls were hard workers and just as capable as any man when riding horses and moving cattle. "Six girls," he said, correcting himself. He wasn't used to thinking of Reese as his, but now that he knew, he'd have to make sure he never forgot to include her.

Lloyd sat back and sipped his coffee. Did Reese know how to ride? If not, that had to be remedied. He glanced down at his shotgun. She'd need to know how to shoot, too. In his mind, it was a basic survival skill when a person lived in the mountains.

Then his mind went to Sara, and his heart skipped a beat. That girl had been the first love of his life, and then she disappeared. He never understood, but it all made sense now. The only thing that didn't make sense was why she'd stayed silent. He figured they'd have a friendly conversation about it, and then they could both be on their way. He was a widower, still mourning the loss of his wife. Carol had been gone for several years now, but there wasn't a day he didn't miss her. He hadn't been with another woman since. Well, that wasn't exactly the truth.

Lloyd chuckled, thinking about Elsa Buchanan, and how she'd kissed him. He hadn't been kissed like that in years, and it was nice. He would have dated her if he'd been ready to move on. She was a spitfire of a woman. He liked the ones with a mind of their own and a fire in their bellies. They made good conversation, were terrific lovers, and there was never a dull moment. But as the father of six girls, maybe dull was something to appreciate.

Headlights lit up the road as James arrived. Lily walked out the door and stood next to him on the porch. "Be nice to him, Daddy. If you scare this one away, I swear I will make your life miserable."

"More miserable than it already is?" Lloyd chuckled. "If he scares too easily, he's not worthy of your love. I save you lots of time and heartache by weeding the weak out at the beginning."

"Keep telling yourself that if it makes you feel better." She leaned down and kissed his cheek. "I realize you always wanted sons, but just remember that old saying: A daughter is yours for life; a son, only until he takes a wife. Also, remember, when I find a husband, you get a new son." She tapped his head. "Get your head in the right space, Pops." She walked down the stairs and met James halfway.

"Don't fear his shotgun. He won't use it unless you make me unhappy."

Lloyd laughed. His Lily was spirited like her mother. Any man who took her on had his hands full. Come to think of it, all of his daughters were like their mother. He probably didn't have to worry so much about them, but he was their father, and that was his job. He rolled to his feet as James approached.

"Good morning, sir. Thank you for inviting me out to clean your stalls." James eyed the gun leaning against the house. "You should know I'm not afraid of your show of force, and I'm less afraid of hard work."

Lloyd shook his hand, then walked down the stairs and turned toward the stables.

The door opened, and Basil ran out. "I'm here."

"Barely." Lloyd looked at James, who was keeping up with his double-time pace. "Have you met my boy, Basil?"

"It's Baz, Dad. I keep telling you I go by Baz."

Lloyd reached out and cuffed his son upside the head. "Your birth certificate says Basil. Your mother named you that, and that's what I'll be calling you. What the hell is Baz? It sounds like spaz." He rubbed his chin. "You know what? You might be on to something there. If you can change your name, so can I. Meet my son, Spaz. He gets up at two minutes to six for a six o'clock show time to work."

James shrugged. "At least you know he can be ready at a moment's notice. It's that way in the station too. We set our gear up at night so if the alarm rings, we can be ready in seconds flat. I'd say it's an excellent skill." He looked at Lloyd and must have seen the frown. "But your father is right. You should give yourself more time. My granny used to say, 'Early is on time, and on time is late.'"

"Are you kissing up to our father?" Basil asked.

"Yes, I am. I'm not stupid." He walked beside Lily toward the stables. "I want to date your sister, and the only way that's happening is if I gain your father's favor."

"Finally, a man who knows the drill," Lloyd said.

They entered the stable, and Lloyd turned on the lights which hummed to life. The horses moved in the stalls, with a few poking their heads over the gates to see the commotion.

"You know anything about horses, son?" Lloyd asked James.

"I can ride one, but that's about all."

"That's a start." He looked at Lily. "Show your ..." What did he call James? Was he Lily's boyfriend, or was she trying him out? He knew nothing about dating in this day and age. "Show James the morning routine while I saddle Hellion."

He needed to make sure his horse was okay. Basil had pulled in the horses at the first sign of bad weather, but Hellion spooked and cut his leg on something. Lloyd had cleaned up the wound and wrapped it, but Hellion favored the leg. A ride might loosen the stiffness in the joint where the injury occurred.

"Basil, you and Rose are moving the cattle to pasture two." He grabbed his saddle and walked toward Hellion's stall. "Family meeting at five in the kitchen. Oh, and before I forget, we're having guests for dinner. Poppy is coming too and will help prepare."

Lily smiled. "Can James come?"

Lloyd looked at the two of them together. His daughter was all doe-eyed, and James was a smiling goofball. "He ain't family."

Lily stomped her boot. "Not to the family meeting, but dinner. I swear, if it were up to you, we'd all die spinsters."

"Not true." He figured it was coming out one way or another, and if James were a keeper, he wouldn't mind a minor family scandal. Hell, if he'd listened at Doc's, he already knew and proved he could follow orders and keep a secret. "He can come if he can put in a full day's work. We aren't a charity, and everyone earns their keep."

"That must be some dinner," James said.

"It's chicken, but in your case, you're investing in the company you keep, and right now, that's my daughter Lily, and there is nothing cheap about her."

"Yes, sir. Where do we start?"

While Lily and James moved the other horse from the stable to run loose in the paddock, Lloyd saddled Hellion. The wound on his right front leg was healing, but he was still babying it.

"Hey, boy. Let's take a ride. You can use the workout, and I can use the time to clear my head." He had to find a way to deal with Sara. It took all he had not to go to the beach house and knock on her door the last few days. Half of him wanted to yell and scream and rail, but the other half wanted to hug her. The want-to-hug-her half was winning.

His mind went back to the day he found her car down the embankment. His heart lurched into his throat. He had to give her credit. She was one tough cookie. Most women hanging from their seatbelt with a bloody gash on their head would have been in hysterics. Sara was merely inconvenienced.

While he was sympathetic to her accident and injury, she had a lot to answer for. They'd had a child together. Not together, but Reese was his, and he needed answers as to why she didn't tell him.

He searched his memory for the last time he laid eyes on her. It was when she approached him at the beach. At that time, he was visiting a friend with Carol, who was pregnant with Poppy. Oh, the look on Sara's face when she got to them. It was like he'd been cheating on her and got caught. That saying about a woman scorned was true, but he hadn't left her and married another. She left him and said nary a word for years and then showed up and acted all mad that he'd moved on. He introduced her to Carol and told her they were having a girl named Poppy.

Hellion walked stiffly to the pasture, but once he was there, the horse cantered as if letting the breeze blow his mane would take all the cares in the world away. With his foreman, Jimmy, at a cattle auction, Lloyd rode the fence for all day, letting nature and its miracles soothe his worried soul. Obviously, Hellion knew something he didn't about releasing stress, anxiety, and pain.

As he neared the stables, that nervous feeling seeped back into his soul. Would his other children accept Reese as easily as Poppy had? Would Reese accept them? She was a city slicker, and they were as country as it came. Never had he considered what people thought of him or his family, but Reese mattered. What she thought of him mattered. She didn't know him, and he didn't know what Sara had told her. Then there was Sara. Everything circled back to her. What she thought about him mattered too. What he couldn't figure out was why it did?

He took care of Hellion and entered the house to find all of his kids sitting in the living room waiting for him. Everyone had a grim look on their face but Poppy.

"You're not dying, are you?" Basil asked.

Lloyd took the empty recliner and sat on the edge with his elbows on his knees and his chin resting on the knuckles of his interlaced fingers. "No, I'm fine."

"Why are we here?" Daisy asked. "The last time you called a family meeting was when mom was dying. You don't call these kinds of meetings unless something is wrong."

She had a point, and he hated that he alarmed them. "I called this meeting because I have information to share. It may shock you, and I wanted to have you all in the same place so I could answer questions that may come up."

Violet, the youngest of his daughters, started crying. "You're sick. Oh my God. I knew it. It's why he hasn't met anyone since mom passed. He's dying and doesn't want to burden them with the anguish of losing him." She was always the most dramatic of his children so it didn't surprise him that she thought the worst.

"I'm not dying. I need to talk to you about something big, and I don't know how to start."

"I'll take care of it." Poppy stood. "Dad had a baby with another woman, and she's surfaced recently." Poppy basically shook a soda can, popped the top, and it all came spewing out.

Gasps came from all over the room. "Did you have an affair?" Rose asked.

Lloyd stood and pointed to Poppy and then the chair. "Okay, let's get this under control. Blurting it out isn't helping. I did not have an affair. Sara was my first love, and we ... well ... we had a daughter."

Basil groaned. "Another girl? Isn't my life a living hell as it is with five sisters? And now I have six." Throw pillows sailed through the air to hit him in the head. His girls had perfect aim.

Lloyd stuck his thumb and index finger in his mouth and let out a whistle that silenced the room. "My best guess is Reese was born five years before Poppy. I knew nothing about her until this week. Her mother, Sara, is in town as well."

Lily raised her hand as if asking permission to talk, which was odd because Lily did what she wanted. "Are you going to date her again?"

Lloyd immediately shook his head. "No, I'm not. What your mother and I had was special. I'm not looking to replace her."

"You know, Dad," Daisy said. "No one expects you to stay single and celibate for the rest of your life. Even Mom told you to find someone new, but I'm sure she wouldn't mind if you had someone old."

"Sara is not old. She's my age." His kids looked at each other and smiled. "Don't get any funny ideas. I'm not interested in her. Besides, you don't start a relationship with lies, and she kept Reese from me all these years."

"Have you found out why?" Lily asked.

"No, but I plan to find out everything," Lloyd answered.

Basil cleared his throat. "When do we meet her?"

"Them," Lloyd corrected. "You meet them at dinner tonight." He looked at his watch. "I imagine they will be here soon." He turned to Lily. "Where's your boyfriend?"

Lily smiled. "James went home to change. Do you like him?"

"He's okay. Let's see if he eats with his mouth closed." Lloyd wasn't known to be easy on his daughters' dates, but he had to admit James might be one of the better choices he'd seen lately. He was gainfully employed. The stables were clean. And the young man was respectful. The best thing he had going for him was being a local.

Lily had a year left at ASU, and then she'd have to decide where she'd take that engineering degree. Maybe falling in love with an Aspen Cove firefighter wasn't such a bad idea. All he'd ever wanted was a big family all in one place. If James was here and Lily was in love with him, then she'd return once she graduated.

"Are there any questions about what we discussed?"

Daisy stood. "I'm sure there are thousands. It should be an interesting dinner." She looked at her siblings. "You know the drill. We need to get this house in tip-top shape in fifteen minutes." She clapped her hands together, and everyone assumed some predetermined position to tidy up. She pointed at him. "Go shower because you smell like your horse. Wear that blue plaid shirt you've got hanging in your closet for special occasions and your best jeans."

"You understand this is about integrating the families, right? We aren't matchmaking."

"I know what you need. Just trust me, okay?"

Lloyd walked up the stairs. "Not for a moment."

CHAPTER FIVE

It had been three days since the accident. Three days where her daughter hovered over her like a Chinook. Reese always accused Sara of helicoptering around her as a kid, but she didn't get what that truly meant until now.

"Did you take your pain meds?" Reese stood at the doorway to the kitchen holding a bottle of ibuprofen and a glass of water.

She wondered how she could get out of going to dinner at Lloyd's and feigning a headache was perfect. "Reese, I don't think I'll go with you tonight." Sara glanced up at her daughter and smiled from her place on the sofa.

"You have to go." She walked into the room and handed over the glass of water and bottle of pain reliever. "Lloyd invited you and gave me direct orders to make sure you came along. I will not disappoint my father by denying him the only thing he's asked of me."

Sara stared out the beach-house window, and a bird swooped down on the water's glass-like surface to pluck a fish from its depths. Until a few weeks ago, she was happily swimming around her pond in Oklahoma, and then Reese got a wild hair up her butt to change ponds and visit Aspen Cove. Sara tried to talk her out of it, but there was no changing her mind. With Reese's stutter and reclusive tendencies, Sara wasn't worried about Aspen Cove's influence on her daughter, but she never imagined the love of a man could change all of that. She was the fish and Lloyd the bird.

"Honey, you don't need me there. Go and have fun." The knot in her stomach tightened.

Reese took a seat next to her mom. "Mom, I need you. I'm asking you to go with me. I know this is scary, but you owe me this. You kept me away from my family all these years. The least you can do is to be there when I meet them."

Sara sat up. "They are not your family. I'm your family. I birthed you and raised you." A tear slipped down her cheek. Thankfully, it was on her left side, and Reese couldn't see it from her position.

"Biologically, I have a father and six half-siblings. It's overwhelming to go from being an only child to one of seven."

Sara sighed. "You are an only child. You are my child." She opened the bottle and took out two pills and chased them with the glass of water before setting the glass and bottle on the coffee table.

Reese took her mother's hand. "I know you're Sc-c-cared. So am I."

She hated that her selfishness and fear were affecting her daughter's speech. Reese hadn't stuttered since Sara arrived, so it had to be her influence over her daughter. Maybe it was she who brought it on the whole time. She'd been told more than once she was a hard taskmaster and expected a lot from those around her, but if she set the bar high, people would rise to reach it. *God, I sound like my mom. How horrifying.*

"I'm not scared. I'm just not interested in spending my evening with a bunch of people I don't know. Besides, I have a headache." She didn't but Reese didn't know that.

"Okay, you can spend the evening by yourself, wondering every second what people are thinking and saying about you. Don't imagine for a second you won't come up. You're why I'm thirty-two and meeting my father and his family for the first time." Reese stood. "I'll tell them you'd lost your mind as a young girl and was convinced storks brought all babies. Let's forget about the pregnancy and the birth abroad." Reese cocked her head. "Speaking of which, does my birth certificate say I was born in France?"

Sara lowered her head. "No." If this kept up, she would have a headache. "Your grandfather was well connected and arranged for a US birth certificate. I used those connections to have it corrected again. I righted that wrong immediately."

"Now it needs to be corrected again because 'father unknown' doesn't really tell the truth."

"It's just a birth certificate."

"No, it's proof I exist, but it's not complete. I need my birth to make sense. It was such a tragedy," Reese said. "I was thinking about it and you have more in common with Lloyd's kids than I do. You lost a parent—both parents. You'd probably feel less of an outsider than I do. Besides, aren't you a little curious? That ranch would have been your life if Grandpa and Grandma hadn't intervened."

Sara had to confess to being slightly intrigued. What would her life have been like had she married Lloyd? She laughed it off because those were the fantasies of a teenager. She dreamed of being a mom to several Dawsons and living in an old farmhouse. Though she couldn't ride a horse, she'd provided veterinary care to many.

Anything could happen in dreams, and in hers, she rode her horse Juniper every morning with Lloyd. Had that been Carol's life? They said the life of a rancher is hard, but is it any harder than single parenting a spirited child? Were all Lloyd's children so willful?

A voice inside her head said, find out. "Fine, I'll come, but we aren't staying there all night. This is a quick dinner, and then we're out of there. Deal?" Reese smiled in that "I'm victorious" way, and Sara would give her this win.

"You should wear something nice."

"This isn't a date." Sara rose and started for the bedroom. She'd taken over Reese's room when she'd moved out with Brandon. They were living in the apartment above the bakery. It was no lake house with a million-dollar view, but they were happy. "I'm not going for them, I'm going for you."

Reese tailed behind her. "You're going because you're curious. I have nothing to do with it."

Sara opened the closet and looked through her meager options. "You have everything to do with it. Without you, Lloyd would have been a faded memory."

"These are perfect." Reese reached past her mother to pull out a pair of jeans. "They make your butt look good."

"Really?" Sara hadn't given her butt much consideration over the years. She was no longer curvy in all the right places. Now she was just curvy in all places.

"Yes, and wear that shirt I love so much. The one I gave you with the saying about being a good human. It will remind you to behave yourself."

Sara stepped back as if her daughter had slapped her upside the head. "Why do you insist I'm not nice? Just because I say things you don't like doesn't mean they are unkind. Sometimes the truth hurts, but it always comes from a good place, and it helps you be a better person."

"Okay. So let me help you, then. You need to work on your social game. Do me a favor. When you open your mouth, taste the words before serving them to others."

"There's that writer in you making everything sound poetic. That was a sweet way of saying shut up, Mom."

"No, that's not what I said. I just meant that you should filter your responses. If Poppy asks you if her butt looks big in her jeans, don't say yes if it does. Just say, 'That's a lovely outfit.'"

"I would never."

"Oh, yes, you would. Remember when we went homecoming dress shopping because you were sure I'd get a date? That poor girl who had a date asked if you liked her dress, and you said it looked like something the dog kept under the porch?"

"Well, it did, and I was helpful because she picked that pretty purple one with the satin sash, and I'm sure her date was pleased too. The other dress looked like a tattered patchwork quilt. It would have been fine as a lap blanket, but not for a dance where photographic evidence would remain in the yearbook to haunt you for decades."

"Get changed, and I'll touch up your makeup."

"I told you, this isn't a date. There's no need to change or put makeup on." Sara could pretend it wasn't a date, but that didn't change the facts. At least it was a date for Lloyd's kids to size her up against their mother. She was being ridiculous, but wasn't it a natural response to compare? Comparison had been her companion all her life. At first it was her parents comparing her to every successful non-pregnant teen. Then it was her comparing herself to every veterinary student. There was also Reese, who compared her to all the moms who let their daughters do anything they wanted.

"Stop lying to yourself. You're an Arden, and you don't leave the house unless you're put together. If Grandma were here, she'd have you all dolled up in a dress and heels, but I imagine this is more like a hoedown and not a cotillion, so denim it is." Reese waited for Sara to change and then led her to the bathroom, where she fixed the tear stain and touched up her makeup so her cheeks were pink and her lashes long.

As they finished, Brandon walked in the front door and called out, "You guys ready?" He had come from work and was going to drive them in his cruiser. Sara wondered what had happened to her daughter's car but didn't get a chance to ask since Reese ran out of the bathroom to no doubt accost her man.

Sara stared in the bathroom mirror. Her wound was healing, and only the faintest of bruising remained. Her hair hid her stitches, but she showed signs of wear and tear.

She had many sleepless nights when Reese was sick and worry lines from when she was out past curfew. The lean body she used to have was gone. Instead, she had the curves of a woman. Her skin wasn't as smooth as a baby's bottom, and it was etched with fine lines and age spots. If she were sixteen, they would have been called freckles.

She could stand there and continue picking herself apart, but she didn't want to start the night defeated. You never got a second chance at making a first impression, and she wanted Lloyd's kids to approve of her. If she were honest, she might have wanted Lloyd's approval too. So, she slicked on her favorite pink lipstick and walked toward the front door. It was now or never.

CHAPTER SIX

Lloyd came down the stairs and found all six of his kids behaving themselves in the living room. Even though they were grown adults, that was a rarity. The house smelled like roasted chicken and potatoes. While Carol was a fantastic cook, none of his daughters got that gene, but they could roast a chicken, so it was a safe bet they wouldn't kill their guests.

"What's she like?" Lily asked.

There would be a lot of questions, so he took his seat in his armchair and remembered the Sara he knew. "She was sweet and funny and full of life."

Lily shook her head. "No, I mean Reese. What is she like?"

"She looks like me," he said.

"Oh, the poor thing," Rose said. "I can't imagine you as a woman."

Put that way, Lloyd couldn't either. He was weathered and aged from years in the saddle and sun. He wouldn't wish his skin on anyone, no less a woman. "She's pretty—lots of curly reddish-brown hair and a smile like sunshine. She has a boyfriend," he said with a grumble to his voice.

"For now," Basil said. "All he needs to do is hang around you for a while, and he'll be gone." The girls nodded.

"I'm not that bad. I'm protective, but I'm a man, and I know how we behave and ... well ... we can be idiots. I'm merely idiot-proofing your love life." He'd always been protective of his girls, but that got worse after Carol died. All they had was him, and he was a poor substitution for their mother, but he tried his best.

Poppy leaned forward. "We love you, Dad, but you raised us, and we know a lot about idiots. Don't forget, Basil is our brother." All the girls laughed while Basil frowned. "Besides, Mom was no pushover. She taught us well." Poppy pointed to herself. "I didn't do bad with Mark, and Lily looks like she chose wisely. You should worry less knowing we had excellent role models."

She was right, but it didn't stop him from worrying. He turned to his son. "What about you?"

Basil lifted his chin. "I like my women wise and kind and strong." Under his breath, he said, "And older."

Daisy laughed. "Mrs. Brown is available."

Lloyd didn't understand his son's obsession with older women, but a man liked who he liked. As he thought about that, he came to the disturbing conclusion that he'd treated Basil far differently than he had his daughters. He could almost feel Carol giving him a pinch and telling him to wake up and move into this century.

His ears perked up at the sound of tires crunching on the gravel driveway. His stomach flipped and flopped. There was much to be excited about and a lot to internalize. Reese would be a blessing in his life, but he wasn't so sure about Sara. She didn't seem pleased at the suggestion to spend time with him. He rose from the chair and walked to the door. When he opened it, there were three cars. The first was James'.

"Lil, your boyfriend is here." Lily whooped and ran out the door, throwing herself into James' arms. Someone needed to talk to her about her enthusiasm. The next one was Mark, who walked over and shook Lloyd's hand before stepping inside to kiss Poppy. Lloyd had to admit that while Mark's father had done his family wrong, holding that grudge as he did all those years served no one well, especially Poppy. And after losing Carol, he recognized how much time he'd wasted for his daughter and son-in-law by refusing to allow them to date. When you loved someone, you needed to spend all your minutes letting them know it because one day, they'd be gone, and all that remained were the memories.

Brandon stepped out of the third car, a sheriff's cruiser. Every city-owned car was in his driveway. Either they had better luck than the rest of the town when it came to the storm, or they were better protected during it.

The newest deputy rushed around to the passenger side to help Reese out before opening the back door to assist Sara. Lloyd was so tuned into them, he didn't notice his entire clan had come out of the house and stood on the porch. Sara, Reese, and Brandon crept forward as if walking toward their demise.

He stepped off the porch and met them halfway. "Welcome to the ranch." He pointed at his family. "This is the Dawson clan. Let me introduce you to your brother and sisters." He looked at Sara, whose pinched expression told him everything. Obviously, she didn't like the idea of Reese having a family other than her. The funny thing was, she'd always had them.

He leaned over and whispered to Sara. "Thank you for coming. I know this isn't easy." He tried to put himself in her place and couldn't imagine what was going through her head. "I'm not trying to take her from you. I'm only trying to have a part of her for myself." He moved ahead of them and stood by Poppy. It was funny how his kids lined up in order of birth. "This is Poppy." Poppy hugged an oof out of Reese. As he went down the line, the others were gentler but no less enthusiastic. "Shall we go inside?" The kids entered first, along with their significant others, leaving Sara and him last.

She glanced down at the shotgun leaning against the wall. "Is this always out here?"

He shook his head. "Only when there are boyfriends around."

She laughed. "Does it work?"

He held the door for her. "It must. I haven't had to shoot anyone yet."

As they walked inside, he looked at his home through fresh eyes. Carol kept telling him their house was worn and needed some upgrades. But he came from the camp that said, *if it ain't broken, then don't fix it.* However, as he took in the furniture, paint, and curtains, he had to agree with his late wife. His home was tattered and in need of some upgrades.

The hardwood floors were scuffed, and a pattern from the front door to the stairs was etched into the surface. The walls were a dingy white and covered with family photos. The furniture was in good shape, but it was leather, and the older it got, the softer it became. It was also faded where people sat.

"Welcome to our home." He pointed to the living room. "Have a seat. I think dinner will be ready in a little while." He offered Sara his chair, and all his kids stared, but when he glowered at them, they turned their attention to Reese, who'd taken a seat beside Brandon on the couch.

"Is this weird for you?" Rose asked.

Reese nodded. "Y-y-yes." Brandon squeezed her hand, and she leaned into him. "I s-stutter when I'm n-nervous."

Violet sat on the other side and placed her hand over Reese's shoulder. "You don't have to be nervous. We're family."

"Thank you."

Daisy pointed to Brandon. "You're lucky you came with a boyfriend. Otherwise, Dad would have made that poor man run through the gauntlet to date you."

"I'm sure he'll test me." Brandon looked at Lloyd. "Isn't that right, sir?"

Lloyd nodded. "I've got my eye on you, but I like what I see. I don't imagine it was easy getting past Sara. She seems to have a good handle on things." He figured it wouldn't hurt to give her credit for the daughter she'd raised.

Sara looked at Lloyd before turning to Reese. "She snuck him in when I wasn't looking, but I like him, too. He was a soldier. That says something about loyalty and commitment. He's also a gentleman, which is hard to find these days." She eyed all the girls one by one. "Being an independent woman doesn't mean you can't let a man open the door, bring you flowers, and give up his seat for you. You can still rule the roost and get all that. Whoever tells you that you can't have everything is a liar."

Reese smiled. "Did I tell you I love your shirt, Mom?"

Sara leaned back and frowned.

"I agree with your mother. Strong women are an asset to this world." Lloyd laid his hand on Sara's shoulder. At first, she stiffened, and then she relaxed under his touch. "Is dinner ready?"

Rose and Poppy went straight to the kitchen. "Yes, let's eat."

"Can I help?" Reese asked.

Lily took her hand. "You and I can pour drinks. We've got lemonade or iced tea. There's also coffee. Why don't you take the orders, and I'll pour."

"Deal," Reese said.

All the kids, and their significant others left the living room to complete their assigned tasks, leaving Sara and him alone.

"That started well," he said.

"You have a lovely family." She rose and went straight for the wall of memories where pictures of Carol were intermixed with the kids. "Your wife was beautiful. I'm sorry for your loss."

He stared at the center photo, Carol dancing in a field of wild sunflowers. "She was a good woman."

"I'm glad you were happy."

"I would have been happier had I known, Sara."

She inhaled deeply and let it out with a sigh. "It was a complex situation."

"We have to talk about it at some point."

"I know, but we're going to eat right now."

He led her to the dining room and pulled out the chair beside him. This would be the first time someone sat in Carol's chair. He looked at his kids, who were already seated at the large rectangular table. None of them appeared bothered that another woman was in their mother's place. Not that Sara was taking Carol's place. He wasn't interested in building a relationship with anyone. At least that was the lie he'd told himself. If he were honest, he was lonely and missed long walks and deep talks and the intimacy of having a partner.

"What are we waiting for? Pass the food," Basil said.

Lloyd held up his hand. "Maybe our guests say grace?"

Sara shook her head. "Only on special occasions."

Lloyd held out his hands and took Reese's and Sara's. "This is a special occasion." He said a short prayer, giving thanks for the food and family and for getting a chance to meet his daughter. "Pass the chicken," he said.

The next hour was spent eating and talking. Poor Reese was bombarded by questions about everything in her life from birth until today.

"You write romance?" Poppy asked.

"I do, but as a ghostwriter, I don't get credit for any of the words."

"But she's going to write under her real name from now on." Brandon had a big smile on his face. It wasn't hard to see how proud he was of Reese.

"I'd like your permission to use Dawson as a nom de plume." Reese gripped the edge of the table but didn't take her eyes off him. It was as if she were bracing herself for a letdown.

"What's a nom de plume?" he asked

"My pen name. The name I'd use as a writer."

Lloyd smiled. "Reese Dawson. That sounds like a bestselling author."

AFTER THE MEAL, the kids suggested a game. There was no better way to welcome someone into the family than with a cut-throat game of Monopoly.

Sara lifted her hand into the air to get Reese's attention. "We agreed to go home after dinner."

Reese looked at her mom, and her shoulders sagged. "You're right. I'm sorry." She rose from her seat to the sound of groans from her siblings.

"How about I take you home?" Lloyd followed Sara's gaze to Reese, who was pleading with her beautiful green eyes to stay.

As moments passed, Sara was torn but eventually she nodded. "Thanks, Lloyd. That would be wonderful." She touched her head. "I'm still not myself after that accident."

Sara said goodbye to his kids and hugged Reese, telling her she'd see her soon before she followed Lloyd out the door to his truck.

He opened the passenger door and gave her a boost into the seat. "Buckle up. It's a bumpy ride."

He rounded the truck, took a seat behind the wheel, and then turned to her. "Again, thank you for coming. Now that we're alone, do you want to tell me your story?"

CHAPTER SEVEN

"I don't know where to begin." She looked out the window as they drove down the road. It was still daylight but quickly moving into dusk. "Our entire relationship started on a lie."

"What do you mean, it started on a lie? I never lied to you." He trudged along the winding dirt road, heading into town. "I told you I loved you, and I meant it."

The trees passed by. First one, then another. It reminded her of the years that had gone by since that day they first made love. In her 16-year-old brain, it was love, but looking back, she wasn't sure. Those were words confessed during the heat of passion. Endorphins did funny things to the mind and body.

So much had happened that summer. Even now, she couldn't get her mother's voice out of her head. She'd called her everything but a whore. She didn't need to use the words because she'd insinuated it repeatedly.

After a deep breath, she let out a sigh. "No, I lied to you. When my parents absconded with me back to Oklahoma, I was sixteen and pregnant."

He tapped the brakes, and they jolted forward. "Sixteen! What do you mean you were sixteen? You told me you were eighteen."

She shrugged. "I lied." What was done was done. There was no reason to be dishonest now. "If I had told you I was underage, you would've never given me a second glance. I wanted to be with you so badly that I stretched the truth. I didn't want you to think of me as some silly, infatuated girl." She leaned against the window, hoping the cool glass would help calm her frazzled, heated nerves. "That summer was the best and worst of my life."

"Jesus, Sara. I could have gone to jail because you lied." His hands gripped the steering wheel so tightly that his knuckles blanched. "What were you thinking?"

"I didn't start off trying to deceive you. I fell in love, and once my heart was involved, I would've done anything to keep you." Lloyd was the first person who loved her for her—not her potential. She never needed to be anything but herself with him. Well, that wasn't exactly true. She needed to be two years older.

"Anything but tell the truth."

"That's not fair. I was sixteen."

"But in my mind, you were eighteen, which doesn't make you any more mature than a sixteen-year-old. However, at least at eighteen, you were legal. And now you're telling me you left Aspen Cove, went back to Oklahoma, and found out you were pregnant. Why didn't you tell me?"

She threw her hands into the air. "Don't you get it? I couldn't tell you. Do you remember the day I got the flu, or I assumed it was the flu? I was pregnant. I got the test at Doc's pharmacy and took it. In hindsight, I should have told you first, but I didn't. I told my mother who had visited that weekend."

"And she what? Spirited you away and locked you in a closet for decades?"

"That's close. You met my parents. They were uppity and tidy and full of themselves. I was lucky I wasn't sent to a convent. In fact, that was thrown out there. But, in the end, I had two choices regarding our baby. I could give her up for adoption or have her and pretend my mother gave birth to her overseas. I refused to lose our child, so I took option two, and for a time, Reese was raised as my sister. It was okay to have an oops baby in our circles, but it wasn't okay to have a child out of wedlock as a teenager. So, to keep our daughter, I had to agree to never talk to you again, never see you, and never tell you because you would complicate things. My options were limited. I chose the one where I could keep her, and in keeping her, I got to hold on to a piece of you." She turned away from him and stared out the window.

Lloyd drove the rest of the away to the beach house in silence. He pulled into the driveway, turned off the engine, and shifted his body to face her. "This is a far longer conversation than a quick ride home allows. Can I come in?"

She faced him and rolled her shoulders to release the tension. This was the conversation she was supposed to have with him twenty-seven years ago on the beach when she came back to town. She owed him more than a simple answer, but she had nothing else to say that would add anything to the conversation.

"That's the gist of it. I had Reese, and we all pretended she was my parents' child in public. In private, she was mine. I birthed her, changed her, fed her, and cared for her physical and emotional needs. My parents took care of her financial needs. As you know, kids are expensive. There isn't anything else to say."

He opened his door. "You're wrong. We've got thirty-two years to catch up on. I've missed all that time with her, and you owe me information." He stepped out of the truck and rounded the front to open her door. "I won't force myself in, but I'd like more time with you."

Her heart skipped a beat when he said those words. They had nothing to do with her, but the teenage girl still trapped inside let her heart gush with warmth. The grown woman she'd become tucked that feeling aside because any time Lloyd wanted to spend together came from his need to know about Reese and nothing more.

She got out and walked toward the door. "Come on in. I've got a bottle of wine. Let's pop it open and sit on the deck. If you want thirty-two years, it's going to take alcohol." She opened the door and headed straight for the kitchen, where she pulled a bottle of cabernet from the rack.

"Grab two glasses from the last shelf on your left." She got the opener and the wine and waited for him to get the glasses. When he was beside her, she led him out the back door and onto the deck, where she took a seat in one of the Adirondack chairs. She never understood her brother Frank's love of those chairs. They were basically pine chair prisons. Once you got in one, it was nearly impossible to get out because they were so low to the ground. Add in some wine and she would have to roll out onto her knees and crawl to the rail to hoist herself to standing again.

He removed the cork from the bottle and poured them each a glass. "I'm sorry you didn't think you had a choice. I would have supported you and Reese. I'd like to think I'm a good man. I always try to do the right thing."

She smiled at him. "You were a nice boy."

He chuckled. "I'm a rancher. We grow up fast. At eighteen, I was more of a man than someone at thirty or forty. Life is hard on the ranch. You know the saying, early to bed and early to rise makes a man healthy, wealthy, and wise. I wouldn't say I'm rich, but we do okay." He inhaled a breath and let it out with a whoosh. "I wish you would have told me."

She sipped her wine and looked over the lake. The slight breeze caused tiny ripples to travel across its surface. Several ducks swam near the shore, with the ducklings following close behind. She considered parenthood among species of all types. Except for penguins, almost every species left the children solely in the mother's care. In her case, she was raised by staff, but they were mostly women who nurtured her when allowed.

"It's not that I didn't think you'd step up. I wasn't given the choice to see if you would."

He leaned back in the chair and kicked his booted feet in front of him. Lloyd was tall with long legs. She rather liked his rugged look. She had thought about him over the years and couldn't imagine what he'd look like as a mature man, but in her mind, it wasn't this. He was quite handsome. She might even say he got better with age, like a good wine.

"Why wait all these years?"

There were so many reasons, but the truth sounded so lame. "I was protecting you."

He took several deep breaths before taking a drink of his wine. "How does keeping me in the dark about my flesh and blood protect me?"

She tried to put herself in his shoes. What if the tables were turned, and she'd never known Reese? Part of her wanted to chuckle because she was reasonably sure that would be fine with her daughter, but on her side, she couldn't bear giving Reese up. She was all Sara had.

Sure, there was Frank, but he was married to his job. For family—real family, the kind you'd give an organ to—she only had Reese. And as hard as she was on her, it came from a place of love. She only wanted what was best for her daughter. Once again, she sounded like her mother.

"After my parents passed, the first place I came was here. I had this fantasy that I'd show up, and you'd be here pining for me after all those years."

"It was five years without a word. I assumed I was a summer fling, and you forgot about me."

She drank her wine in three gulps and poured herself another glass. "Hard to forget you when I looked into your eyes each day."

"You could have called."

"You forget, there weren't cell phones in every pocket thirty years ago. I had no way to reach you except for a landline or mail. I didn't know if you were still at the ranch. I had to accept that there might be someone else even though I'd hoped there wasn't." Even in her early twenties, she was naïve and a romantic. She'd had so many fantasies about that day and it turned out to be a nightmare.

He leaned back and closed his eyes. "I remember that day well. I didn't know what to do. My heart was torn." He opened his eyes and looked at her, and his heart was still torn. "Here was my first love, running toward me like a clip out of a movie, arms spread, with a smile on your face. You were relieved to see me, and I was stunned to see you."

She attempted to sit forward, but the chair's angle forced her back. After several tries, she gave up and leaned against the stiff wood. "I was relieved. I came here to find you. I didn't expect the universe to deliver you to me, but there you were. I was there to tell you about Reese."

"But you didn't."

She shook her head. "No, because when I got there, I came face to face with your reality." She made a rounded motion with her hand over her belly. "And she was very pregnant. You sidestepped me and reached down to help her up. When you introduced her as your wife, my world came crashing down. You said you were having a girl and naming her Poppy. Carol looked so happy and proud."

She looked up at the sky and bit her lower lip. Then she brought her gaze down to him. "And in that second, I promised myself I wouldn't take something away from her or you. In Carol's mind, she was giving you your first child. Imagine me blurting, 'Oh, by the way, I left our five-year-old down the beach with Bea's daughter. Oh, and guess what, we don't know it yet, but she will jump out of Bent-over-Betty and nearly drown while I'm accusing you of moving on too quickly.'" A tear slipped from her eye. "Can you imagine that? I made a snap decision to shut up. I said hello, and I ran away."

"Wait. Reese nearly drowned?"

Another tear fell. "Not nearly. She drowned, and no one knows who pulled her from the water, but my guess is Brandy did, and then she ran in to get Bea's help. I lost you for good that day, but I almost lost her, too. After she got stitched up, I packed up and went back to

Oklahoma, where we stayed until Reese got a wild notion that coming to Colorado would be good for her creativity."

"Was she okay after that?"

She had relived that day at least a hundred times in her mind. In her attempt to find love, she nearly lost the only thing she'd truly cared for in her life. From that day on, she turned into her mother.

"Every traumatic event has a lasting impact." Her pregnancy had changed her for all time and eternity. No one comes out of life unscathed. "Until then, she was fearless. I couldn't keep enough Band-Aids on hand for the scrapes and bruises she got trying everything. The girl didn't know the word no, but after that day, she was scared, and my vibrant, beautiful girl turned inside herself. Before that, you couldn't shut her up, but she couldn't string a sentence together after that day. She stuttered nonstop, and then because I'd get frustrated with her and finish her sentences, she stopped speaking altogether." Each time Reese stuttered was a reminder of how she'd failed her daughter.

She swiped at the tears freely flowing down her cheeks. "I was an awful parent. Talk about protective. Because I'd failed her when I ran to you, I was all over her for the next twenty-seven years, like lint on tape. No wonder she ran away and came here." Setting her wine down on the arm of her chair, she buried her head in her hands and wept.

He reached over and patted her back. "She seems okay now."

A bubble of laughter rose to the surface and let loose. It sounded more like a haunted cackle. "That's the thing. She wasn't okay until she came here and met Brandon. Did you know he was a hitchhiker she picked up on the side of the road?"

Lloyd sat up straight. "She had to know better than that. You taught her about stranger danger, right?"

"Don't blame me. Of course, she knew better, but she told me the story of how they met, and what could I say? What was done was done. Then Doc got involved and called in a favor from Frank.

Brandon was supposed to stay at B's Bed and Breakfast, but the new owner was sick, so he stayed with Reese."

"And now they're living together? Surely, you taught her better than that?"

"Why are you blaming me?"

"Because you raised her. If I had raised her, he would have met my shotgun before taking her on her first date. You were way too lenient with her."

Sara's jaw dropped. "You don't get to come over here and armchair parent. You weren't there. You don't get to second guess my decisions."

"And whose fault is it I wasn't there?" His voice echoed through the air.

"It wasn't mine," she said. "Haven't you heard a word I said?"

He stood up and stared down at her. "I heard you loud and clear, but it was me who had no choice."

"Neither did I."

He shook his head. "You talk about our daughter not knowing the word no, but I recall a young woman who was just as headstrong. The Sara I knew wouldn't have accepted the word no either."

"That Sara wasn't pregnant."

"Oh, yes, she was. She just didn't know it, and when she did, she caved."

"That's not fair. I was a young girl."

"Oh, I know now. You were sixteen, and I had no business being with you." He shoved his hands in his pockets and paced the length of the deck. "I don't even know why I'm here now. Everything I want to know about Reese, I'll get from the horse's mouth."

"You do that." She tried to get up again but fell back into the chair. "But while you're at it, try not to be a horse's ass."

Lloyd let out a breath that sounded like a neigh. "Good luck to you, Sara. I wish you well." He walked to the stairs and took them two at a time. The man couldn't get away from her fast enough.

As he turned the corner, she gulped the rest of her wine and yelled, "I hope your horse twists an ankle and throws you from the saddle, you big oaf. Who do you think you are?" She rolled to her knees and crawled to the rail to pull herself up. She looked at the almost-empty bottle and walked inside to get another. After tonight, she'd need one.

CHAPTER EIGHT

"Who does she think she is?" Lloyd mumbled on his way to the truck. He situated himself behind the wheel and pulled out of the driveway. "How dare she call me a horse's ass." Sara was out of her mind if she thought this was his fault. She lied and then withheld the truth for over thirty years. "Who does that?"

Lloyd was headed home but somehow ended up parked in front of Bishop's Brewhouse. It was probably a good idea to cool off before he faced Reese. Nothing good came from riled emotions. It wouldn't go well for him if he showed up mad at her mother. From his experience, mothers and daughters had solid bonds and saying anything negative about Sara wouldn't reflect kindly on him. It didn't matter if Sara was in the wrong. All that mattered was she was Reese's mom. Blood was thicker than water, and right now, he was water until he proved he deserved to be family.

He parked the car and entered the bar. It had been years since he'd been inside. The last time was for Bea's memorial service when Doc handed out pink envelopes. He never got one, but he didn't expect one either. Those envelopes went to needy people, and he wasn't a needy man.

His life fell apart when Carol died, but he got up each morning, pulled on his boots, and went to work. The sameness of that routine helped him through the most challenging time of his life. Somehow, he didn't think his new situation would work the same way. Carol's absence left a hole in his heart, but Reese's appearance made it overflow. On the other hand, Sara made him want to eat steel and spit nails. In the past, he'd been accused of being as stubborn as a mule and had no problem standing his ground. She brought out the worst in him.

He scanned the bar and found several locals enjoying a drink. Dalton's friends were at the pool table, sharing a pitcher and chatting it up. At the bar sat Doc with a half-empty beer mug. Lloyd took the vacant seat beside him. "Do you mind some company?"

Doc lifted his head and widened his eyes. "Are pigs flying? Did hell freeze over?" He raised a hand to get Cannon's attention. "Get the man a beer, son. Seeing Lloyd in here is almost as exciting as winning the lottery or petting a unicorn." He shook his head. "No, not nearly as good, but the odds are about the same." He pulled out his phone and dialed. When the person on the other end answered, he said, "Lovey, remind me to buy a lotto ticket. There's some strange stuff happening in town. I'll explain later." He hung up and turned to Lloyd. "What brings you in?"

"I guess that would be Sara." Cannon slid him a light beer and walked away. "I don't know where to begin."

Doc chuckled. "We all know where it began—probably the seat of your first truck. The question is, where is it going?"

Lloyd sipped his beer and pondered that question. Where was it going? As far as he was concerned, it wasn't going anywhere. Whatever relationship he had with Sara was over the day she left. "Sara and I don't have a relationship if that's what you're getting at. That ended decades ago. What we have is a common interest—Reese." He watched the condensation on his frosted mug drip down the side like tears. "I made her cry."

"Who?"

"Sara. Are you listening to me or not?"

"There are two women in this conversation. Forgive me if I'm a little confused."

"I made Sara cry." He went back to the conversation in his mind. "I didn't make her, but I brought up a memory that made her cry."

"And how does that make you feel?"

Thinking about it made his heart clench again. "Like hell. I'm a man who's been surrounded by women all his life. With a wife and five girls, I've seen many tears, and every single one has made me feel bad regardless of fault. No man wants to see his girl cry."

Doc lifted one bushy brow and smiled. "Is Sara your girl?"

"No. I just told you we don't have a relationship."

"I heard you." Doc stared at his empty mug and then searched the bar. If he was looking for Cannon, he wouldn't find him nearby because he'd gone down the hallway minutes ago. "If we're going to talk about women. I need more beer." Doc nodded to the taps and slid Lloyd his mug. "Get me a refill, will ya?"

Bishop's Brewhouse had worked on the honor system for as long as he could remember. Cannon didn't care who went behind the bar to pull a beer as long as they paid for what they took, didn't mess with the till, and didn't tease his one-eyed cat, Mike. Lloyd took Doc's mug behind the counter and poured him another light beer.

"I don't want to talk about women. I came here for the silence." It was a lame excuse because no one came to a bar for peace and quiet. Bars were social scenes. He returned to his chair and picked up his beer, looking around the place to see small groups of people chatting and the rowdy group of bikers hooting' and hollerin' over a game of pool. If he wanted silence, he'd come to the wrong place.

"Since you're buying the beer, I figure I owe you a session."

Lloyd smiled. Doc was a legend, and so were his antics. He rarely paid for a beer. He either played tic-tac-toe for it, or he roped someone into buying it by telling them they owed him for the words of wisdom he imparted to them. Beer was a small price to pay for sage advice.

"I'm all ears." He stared at Doc's deeply lined face and white hair. Where had the years gone? He'd known him all his life, yet here sat a man who had aged a thousand lifetimes. Doc sported nearly black hair and the bluest eyes in his younger days. He was quite the looker. Even Lloyd's mom had a secret crush on him, but Doc only had eyes for Phyllis. When she died, a part of Doc had too. But now, looking closer, the man still had fire in his eyes, and Lloyd imagined that came from loving Agatha.

"I don't know where to begin with you. It's been a long time since we had a chat."

"I've been busy. The ranch takes all my time."

"Does it? I always imagined the way we spend our time is a choice." He picked up a napkin and set it down between them. "This here paper is you and the ranch. It's all you have, so it's the entirety of your life. That's not well balanced."

Lloyd shook his head. "Not true. I've got the kids."

Doc rubbed his bushy mustache and smiled. "You think you've got your kids, but they're not yours. They are only on loan to you for a time. Eventually, they run off and make their own lives, and guess where you'll be?" He tapped the napkin. "Right here on the ranch by yourself."

Being alone at the ranch didn't sit well with him. That was never his plan. He and Carol had lots of kids, so they'd be surrounded by family forever. "What are you getting at?"

"Nothing. Before you showed up, I was thinking about my life, and how rich it's been. When my Phyllis died, I focused on my patients. Her death took a lot from me. If you recall, Charlie blamed me for her mama's passing. In her eyes, I should have been able to save her. I was a doctor and had skills, but I didn't have the magic Phyllis needed when she had a brain aneurysm." His shoulders rolled forward. "I lost Phyllis and Charlie all at once. I almost gave up medicine, but it was all I had left, so I stuck with it." He crumpled the napkin and hid it in his palm. "Now, let's say this is you and the ranch. If you take it away, you got nothing."

Lloyd shook his head again. "Not true. I've got my kids."

Doc sighed. "Fine, you can live in that dream world, but mark my words, your kids are growing up and finding love, and eventually, they will have lives of their own. Half of your brood is living elsewhere these days. I hear one of the girls is dating James. Poppy is married to Mark. The others will be gone before you know it. Basil is there, but I don't think he's married to the ranch. All that boy needs is a pretty filly to turn his head, and he's gone too. You and the ranch are all you have left, and that ain't much."

Put that way, it made some sense, but he couldn't imagine the ranch without family. "Cut through the bull, Doc."

"My life was all about the clinic, and then something amazing happened. Sage came into town." Doc picked up another napkin and tore it in half. He pointed to the first piece and said, "This is the clinic." He pointed to the second piece and said, "This is Sage." He tore her half again, and now there were three pieces. "Add in Lydia, and I've got a fuller life."

He ripped the large piece in half. "Agatha entered and brought back Charlie." He continued to tear the pieces and name people who were part of his life. Doc shook his head and whistled. "Meeting that woman was like getting hit by a Mack truck, who kept pulling forward and reversing over me again and again. I wanted to ignore her, but she refused to be overlooked, and it was damn hard to do because she looked cute in those square-dancing skirts. Still, I did my best, but Agatha was persistent. She never relented. The last straw was when she rescued Dalton. He'd taken a spill on the highway and nearly killed himself. She brought him to me to fix. After that, I couldn't get her to leave."

"You wanted her to leave?"

Doc chuckled. "Hell no, I don't know what I'd do without her. She brings joy to my life." He pointed to the largest piece of the napkin. "This is Agatha." He picked up the pieces and let them fall to the bar. "These people bring me joy and happiness, but Agatha brings me more. My life would be less if I were married to the clinic."

Doc picked up his beer and gulped until his mug was empty. He dropped the crumpled napkin he'd held in his palm. "This is you, son. This is the ranch. You can tear it apart, and yes, your kids are pieces. They bring you joy, but they will never bring you what the love of a good woman can."

"What does this have to do with Sara?"

Doc slid from the stool. "Maybe nothing. Maybe everything. All I know is she brought you Reese, and that's no small task."

"Nope, she kept Reese from me all these years. She's my oldest child, and I don't even know her."

Doc nodded. "I'm sure there was a good reason for what Sara did."

He wanted to yell that there was never a good reason to keep a child from their father, but he couldn't. "She was given an ultimatum. Keep the baby and give me up or give up both of us."

Doc made a sound like he was sucking air through his teeth. "That was a mighty hard decision for a young girl. You ever consider that she was keeping you too by keeping Reese?" Doc turned and shuffled toward the door.

Sara had said something similar. Lloyd stared at the pieces of paper on the bar. He picked up the crumpled napkin that was supposed to represent him and shoved it into his pocket. He didn't know what was more troubling. Was it that Reese had been kept from him, or that the woman responsible still pulled at his heartstrings? It had been decades, but there was still a tiny spark that ignited when she arrived. Was it attraction or blazing fury?

CHAPTER NINE

Sara woke to a knock on the door. She rolled out of bed and into her slippers. The pounding continued as she reached for her robe. The only thing running through her mind as she glanced at herself in the mirror was not only did she act like her mother, but she looked like her, too.

On the third set of knocks, she yelled, "I'm coming." That better not be Lloyd at the door. If it was, she might be tempted to murder the man. How dare he blame her for everything? It's not like she got pregnant by herself. It was the only part he was involved in. She wanted to be bitter about the situation, but what good would that do? She couldn't hold him responsible for something he had zero knowledge about.

She flung the door open, expecting to find the tall handsome rancher, but found a man in overalls.

"Good morning, Ms. Arden. I'm sorry to stop by unannounced, but I didn't have a number for you."

She pulled her robe tight and stared at the man who had curly reddish-brown hair. It was like Lloyd's, but not as full or lovely.

"And you are?"

A blush rose to the man's cheeks. "I'm sorry, I should have introduced myself. I'm Bobby Williams."

Sara stared and waited for more information. The name sounded familiar, but she couldn't place him for the life of her. "I'm drawing a blank here."

"Oh, I'm the mechanic. I towed your car from the ditch."

She touched her stitches, which were still sore but healing. Thankfully, her hair fell over her forehead in a way that perfectly hid them.

"Right." She hadn't given her car a lot of thought. Her life had been a whirlwind since that day. First the accident and then the dinner and the fight. Had all of that happened over a few days? "What a nightmare. I apologize. I should have come over to pay you for towing it to your shop. When can I pick it up?" Though she hated to leave Reese in Aspen Cove, she had to get back to her practice.

His brows drew together as his hand came to his chin to rub the smooth skin. "You rolled your car, Ms. Arden. Do you remember what it looked like?"

After a long moment of frowning, she asked, "I know it's not an easy fix, but how bad is it?" She didn't care about the dents and scratches. "I was hoping to get on the road by the middle of the week."

He cocked his head. "Do you remember the accident?" He said the words slowly as if she was having a hard time understanding him.

She pushed back her hair to reveal the stitches. "Hard to forget."

He shrugged. "Seems like that head injury might have scrambled you a bit. Your car is totaled. The frame is fractured and the engine block shot. I came by to let you know it's not fixable. Do you want me to junk it?" He reached into his back pocket and pulled out a paper. "I've written up the report so you can file it with your insurance. Generally, they will accept this, but they might require an adjuster to come up from Copper Creek." He handed her the paper. "Given that most of the cars in these parts are damaged, they may cut their losses and go with my assessment since I'm a certified mechanic."

She let his words soak in for a few seconds. "It's totaled, as in not repairable?"

He leaned in as if to get a closer look at her. "Do you want me to call Doc? You seem to have difficulty understanding what's going on."

She let out a huff. What was wrong with men in this town? She was having a hard time processing, but not because of her injury. Being stuck in Aspen Cove was not part of her plan. "No, I'm fine. It's a lot to take in. Obviously, coming back here wasn't good for me. Nothing good ever came from Aspen Cove." Once the words were out, she regretted them. Most people had a sense of pride about where they lived and, by Bobby's sour expression, she'd offended him.

"I'd disagree. I've got eight wonderful children that were born here. Everything good in my life came from Aspen Cove, starting with my wife, Louise."

"Eight?" She couldn't imagine having that many kids. "Don't you have cable?" That was the only excuse she could imagine for creating so many children. They must have had nothing else to do.

He smiled and stood taller. "We have every channel you can get. Louise and I love kids and decided we'd have them until we couldn't. Our last little blessing, Paul Robert, was born just over a year ago. We named him after Doc Parker." He stood as proud as a rooster. "Is Reese your only child?"

"Yes, how did you know she was mine?"

He looked over his shoulder. "Small town. News travels fast in these parts."

Sara leaned against the doorjamb. The events of last night and this morning zapped her energy. Knowing she was part of the small-town gossip exhausted her. "What else do you know?"

He rubbed his chin again. "Well, I know Reese is yours, and there's something to do with Lloyd fathering her decades ago. That's about it. Stay a few more days, and everyone will know everything about you."

That was an Arden nightmare. The only chin-wagging allowed better come as a compliment or praise. "What do I owe you?"

Bobby shoved his hands into his pockets. "I didn't get to do anything."

"You towed my car."

He nodded. "I'll get paid by your insurance. I took the liberty of getting the information from your glove box. All you need to do is report the accident."

She touched her palm to her forehead. "Maybe I have lost my mind. I forgot to call that in. I'm sorry. I'll get to it today."

"Don't you worry. All things come in their own time." He stepped back and smiled. "I'll see you around. Let me know what you want me to do with the car."

"I will." She watched him drive away in his tow truck. How had her life gone from bad to worse overnight? She was injured, but now she had no car or way of escape. Her stomach grumbled. "And I'm hungry." That was a situation she'd have to rectify right away because she was the kind of girl that went from hungry to hangry in minutes.

She walked back to her room and changed into jeans and a T-shirt. It was a short stroll into town where she'd be able to eat, make a few calls, and visit her daughter. Picking up her purse, she walked out the door.

Hopefully, Reese would tell her what happened when Lloyd came home. The way he had left made her wonder how he acted in front of her daughter. Was he angry? Did he bad-mouth her?

As she headed downtown, she came to terms with the fact that there was nothing she could do to change what had happened, so what did it matter? He wasn't important to her and fixating on him would do her no good. All she needed was an escape plan, and the sooner, the better.

WHEN SHE ENTERED THE DINER, she breathed in the scent of heaven. There was nothing better than pancakes and bacon, and both scents hung in the air like a delicious fog bank.

"Take any seat, and I'll be right with you," the woman with the big smile and orange lipstick said.

Sara looked around the diner and took in the scene. It wasn't full, but at least half the tables were occupied. In the corner was Doc, reading his paper and sipping his coffee. Across from him sat the woman who ran the front counter of the pharmacy. She assumed it was his wife, but she didn't know for sure. It was funny how everyone in here had information about her, but she didn't know a thing about them. A piece of her longed to be a part of a community, but she'd kept herself sequestered for so long, she didn't know how to belong.

She took the seat in front of the window and texted Reese, asking her to join her for breakfast.

On the walk there, she developed a plan. She'd get a meal, borrow her daughter's car, and head back to Oklahoma. Her idea of coming to Aspen Cove and bringing Reese back failed, so she had to go with plan B, and that was to leave as quickly as possible.

The woman with a name badge that read Maisey walked over with a smile and a coffeepot. "Care for a cup?"

Sara turned two over, knowing Reese would want one. "I'll take two."

"Rough night?"

"You have no idea, but the second one is for Reese." Maisey had to know who that was since it was a small town, and nothing got past a soul here.

"She's a lovely girl." Maisey filled up the mugs. "I should say woman, as she's full grown, but everyone younger than me is just a kid. Do you ever feel that way?"

Sara considered her age. "You mean old?"

Maisey leaned in and whispered, "I like to think of myself as mature." The bell above the door rang, and in walked Reese. "Looks like your date is here. Do you need a minute, or do you know what you want?"

"Pancakes and bacon for me, please, and whatever Reese wants."

Maisey smiled. "That apple doesn't fall far from the tree. She always gets what you're having."

Had she raised a mini-me? God, she hoped not.

"Hi, Mom." Reese sank into the chair across from her. "How was your night?"

"Hellish, but that was yesterday. Today is a new day."

Reese beamed. Somehow, her eyes got brighter and her smile wider. "And how is it going so far?"

"Not great, but I'm still hopeful." Did Sara want to know how Reese's night went? She guessed it was the best of her life by her daughter's demeanor. When was the last time she'd put that kind of smile on Reese's face? After some thinking, she knew exactly when. It was last year when she attended a conference. Her absence made Reese ecstatic. "Am I like Grandma?"

Reese doctored her coffee and lifted it to her lips. "I can't say for sure, as my experience was limited to awful dresses and always being in trouble for chewing with my mouth open."

"You were five."

"Says the woman who took over the bad table manner discussions once Grandma was gone."

Sara covered her face with her hands. "I turned into my mother. I'm so sorry."

After several sips of coffee, Reese put her cup down. "I think it's inevitable that we turn into our parents."

"Again, I'm sorry."

"I get it. Grandma raised you to be perfect, and flawless was the bar she set."

Was that how Reese perceived it? "No, honey. I mean, you're right. Your grandmother expected perfection, and I did my best to make her proud, but I never expected that from you."

Maisey dropped off their pancakes and bacon on her way to another table.

Reese moved the slab of butter over the top one and drizzled it with syrup. "You expected a lot from me, and I never failed to disappoint you."

Sara's heart sank. There were so many emotions at play, but the strongest was regret. "You never disappointed me. How could I be unhappy with you? Look at you. You're a beautiful self-made woman. I've seen no one with as much backbone and courage as you. If anything, I was envious of how you navigated your world."

"Really?" she asked. "You were always impatient. You never let me finish a sentence, and you were so bossy."

Sara held up two fingers. "Different issues. I'm sorry about the interruptions. It was so hard for you to come up with the words. I filled in the blanks to help you, but I can see how rude that must have been. I was truly trying to minimize your discomfort and stress."

"You were shutting me up."

She rocked her body back and forth. "That was never the intent. Though you were a chatterbox as a child, and occasionally it got exhausting to listen to you for hours, after the accident, I missed your voice."

"The accident." Reese looked toward the window.

"Worst day of my life." She chuckled. "Maybe not the worst day. That would have been when I told your grandmother I was pregnant."

Reese picked up a piece of bacon. "That couldn't have been easy." She took a bite.

Sara shook her head. "Nothing with your grandmother was easy. Life was regimented and planned. I never had a moment to break free, so I risked something that summer. Little did I know with my sixteen-year-old brain, I'd ruin everything."

"Was I that bad?"

She did it again. She'd mucked up the conversation and reached out to take Reese's hand, squeezing it so she'd know she loved her. "You were amazing. My overprotective posture came from my failures. I've never been good at relationships. I had an awful one with my parents, and then you came, and I was overjoyed." She went back to the fantasy that played out in her brain. "Can you believe I dreamed I'd pick up and move here, and we'd live with your father as a happy family? What was I thinking? I was young and in love."

"You loved him?"

A warm feeling ribboned through her and settled in her heart. Until her return to Aspen Cove, every encounter with Lloyd brought her that feeling. Now, when she thought of him, another emotion rose inside her. Something fiery, that tasted like ashes and regret.

"I always thought it was love, but I'm sure it was a teenage infatuation and a summer fling. There was never a chance for us. If I'm honest with myself, being with Lloyd was a part of my teenage rebellion. His score was a zero on my parents' approval rating."

"But he's such a nice man."

Hearing her say that was like a gut punch. Her inner, selfish child didn't want Reese to like him, but her outer adult had to be happy she did. "I'm sorry I kept him from you. It was never to hurt you or punish him." This was where she had to pull up her grown-up knickers. "It was self-preservation. You were all I had—all I have. I came back after my parents died, and I still had the dream. In my mind, I pictured it all. I'd go to him and tell him about you, and he'd wrap his arms around me and say, 'Welcome home,' as if I'd been away on a long trip. We would ride off into the sunset and live happily ever after. That only happens to the heroines in your books."

Reese squeezed her hand and let go to dig into her pancakes. "That's not true. I got Brandon. I think love hits you when you least expect it. I didn't think I was worthy of love either, and yet, it found me."

Sara's shoulders rolled forward. "I know love isn't in the cards for me. The times I'd steered toward it, my journey ended in disaster. I'll stick to Pertussis Loving and live vicariously through her exploits."

"It's Loving, pronounced like loathing." She laughed. "I hated that name, but it grew on me. How did you know her name? The book isn't out."

Sara's lips lifted. Despite her not knowing, Sara was Reese's most ardent fan. She'd bought every book her daughter wrote. "I read your notes the first night I was at the cabin."

"You're so sneaky."

Sara pushed her plate away. She'd only taken a few bites, but her hungry stomach was filled with emotion. "It's not so hard to notice things when they're right in front of you." The words sounded true, but they were false. She hadn't known how much she'd hurt her daughter all this time. "I'm sorry for all the pain I've caused you."

Reese grinned. "That's okay. When I have kids, I'll probably torture them equally."

"Kids?" Reese was thirty-two, and she could have children, but given her long-term single status, Sara never considered becoming a grandma. It thrilled and terrified her. "Are you pregnant?"

"No, but we're talking about it. We aren't teeny boppers. I only have so many good eggs left."

"In my book, you're a good egg. When you decide, let me know, and I'll come back."

"Come back? What do you mean? I thought you'd stay a while."

This was a new experience. When was the last time Reese wanted her to stay anywhere? Her last recollection was of kindergarten when she had tugged on Sara's shirt and begged her not to go. Sara had tough loved her and pulled away, leaving her daughter in tears. She cried all the way home that day. Adulting was hard.

"I've got the practice to think about, and honestly, outside of you, there's nothing for me here in Aspen Cove. They already have a veterinarian. They don't need me."

"I need you."

Her chest constricted painfully. This felt like kindergarten all over again. "No, you're perfectly fine on your own. You're talented, strong, beautiful, and completely capable of a life without me." The question was ... was Sara capable of a life without Reese? A lump of guilt lodged in her throat. She'd kept her close, not because Reese needed her but because she couldn't imagine life alone. What a foolish mother she'd been. "I need to get back. I came here because I didn't think you were in a good place, but I see you're in the perfect place for you."

"I wish you would stay. Maybe there is a happily ever after for you too. I mean, my dad is single, and you're single. It's possible that your fantasy could play out."

"You keep thinking with your writer's brain, which helps people see through a different lens. As for me, I need to put this behind me. You know me, once I set my mind to something, I do it, and never look back. I need to go, and that brings me to a problem. I need to borrow your car."

Reese stopped with a piece of bacon midway to her mouth. "Mom, the hail took out my windshield and every windshield within a thirty-mile radius. That's why Brandon drove us in the cruiser. I can't get anyone to fix it for over a week."

"How bad is it?" She figured if it wasn't too bad, she could make it to Denver, get it changed there, and continue her trip to Oklahoma.

"I said it was shattered, but in truth, it's gone. There's a massive hole in the driver's side."

"No problem." She whipped her phone from her purse, looked up the nearest car rental company in Copper Creek, and dialed. When she asked for a rental, the person laughed and told her there wasn't a car available for weeks.

She shoved her phone aside and sighed. "Looks like you're stuck with me until I can get a car."

CHAPTER TEN

Lloyd looked at his watch for the third time, wishing the minutes would pass faster. Today he was getting one-on-one time with his oldest daughter, Reese. When he got back from Bishop's Brewhouse last night, the kids were finishing up their game of Monopoly, so he didn't have time to spend with her, but he invited her to come for a ride today.

Reese didn't know how to ride a horse, so he'd have to correct that since she was a Dawson, and any daughter of his needed that skill. He took Lily's horse, Pad, out of the stall and gave her a good brush down. She was a gentle horse that would be a good seat for Reese to learn on.

Gravel crunched under the weight of tires, and his heart raced. On some level, he imagined this was what an interview for a job was like. He'd never applied for a position in his life because he was born and raised on the ranch. Doing something else never occurred to him.

Today, he had a lot of empathy for those in the interview process. He'd put on his best work shirt and made sure his jeans weren't ripped to shreds. It was important for him to pass any test she may have.

He tied Pad's lead to a rail and exited the barn to find a sheriff's cruiser sitting in his driveway. His first instinct was to panic, but when Reese got out all smiles and happiness, his heart calmed. He'd forgotten her car was damaged during the hailstorm. He was one of the lucky ones who still had an intact truck.

Brandon stepped out from the driver's side, dressed in his sheriff's khakis. Lloyd didn't know the young man well, but he got the impression he was a good guy. However, like all men that came around his daughters, he'd be watching him.

"Sir," Brandon said as he stepped forward and offered his hand. "I would have opened her door, but she was out of the car before I could kill the engine."

Lloyd shook his hand and smiled. "The Dawson girls have a mind of their own." He turned to Reese, whose smile was like high-beam headlights. "Welcome back to the ranch, darlin'." He wasn't sure of the protocol. Did he stand still and let her decide how to greet him, or did he lean over and kiss her cheek? Rather than freak her out with his intense need to be a part of her life, he smiled and waited for her to make the first move.

"I'm excited to be here. I always wanted to ride a horse, but my mother would never allow it." She pointed to her boots—fancy red ones with flowers embroidered all over. "I got these from Katie. She's from Texas and said you can't ride a horse properly without a good pair of boots. And while I'm certain these never met a stirrup, I'm happy to have them. They make me feel dressed for the part. You know, like I'm in the right uniform."

He chuckled because he understood exactly what she meant. He glanced down at his good jeans and smiled. Was he wearing the uniform of a dad?

"You're perfect, and Katie is right. Boots are far superior in stirrups than tennis shoes. You need the heel for traction. You'll see." He looked at Brandon. "Are you joining us, son?" Those words reminded him of Doc, who called every man under seventy son.

"No, sir. I'm on duty. Just bringing Reese to spend time with her father." He leaned over and kissed her cheek. "Call me when you're ready to come home."

"Or I can bring her back."

"Just let me know." Brandon walked back to the cruiser and drove away.

"Are you ready to be a cowgirl?"

"I am."

Lloyd led her to the barn and told her the history of the property. How it had been in their family since the first settlers came from Ireland.

"I'm Irish?"

He touched one of her curls and then pointed to his hair. With all the time he spent in the sun, it had turned blonde, but as a kid, he was a ginger.

"Your great-great-grandfather was Irish, but your great-great-grandmother was Scottish. We were destined to have some red in our hair." He walked into the barn where Pad stood patiently waiting. "This is Pad and she belongs to Lily."

"I get it." Reese laughed. "Lily Pad."

He pointed to the stall where Hellion was. Normally, his horse was nudging at the gate to get out. Hellion didn't come by that name because he was laid back. He was still favoring his leg, which concerned Lloyd. He'd put salve on it and wrapped it again that morning, hoping it would heal quickly.

"This is Hellion, aptly named for his bad attitude, but he's been out of sorts since the hailstorm. He scraped himself in the paddock, and he's not feeling his best." Lloyd fully intended to ride him today, but if Hellion wasn't feeling great, he wouldn't cooperate, and that would make Reese's first riding lesson stressful, so he went to the stall next to Hellion's. "This is Titan. He belongs to Basil."

She moved toward the stall. "He's beautiful. Can I pet him?"

"Yep, but always approach a horse from the side so they can see you, and when you reach out to pet them, they like a good rub on the neck or a scratch behind the ear. If a horse backs away from you, it's best to give them space."

He pulled Titan from the stall and walked him to the center of the stable. "You might as well learn how to saddle a horse." He picked up a brush and handed it to her. "You ever get something in your shoe that rubs uncomfortably?" She nodded. "We brush them before we put on the pad and saddle, so that doesn't happen."

"That makes sense."

He showed her how to give Titan a brush down and saddle him. "I've got your horse ready to go." He took Titan's reins and walked to where Pad stood and handed her the reins. "Since we mount from the left, keep to her left and in her sight. She's a sweet girl and will follow you anywhere you lead." They walked out of the stables and past the barn.

"Lily doesn't mind that I'm riding her horse?"

He tied Titan to a nearby post and walked over to where she stood by Pad. "She was excited to share her with you. All the kids are so happy you're here." That was the truth. Though he didn't get to spend much time with Reese yesterday, he got the whole lowdown from the kids when he got home. He heard how witty and wise she was, and even though she lost the game, she was a good sport about it. They were enamored with her.

"I don't want to monopolize your time or overstep my boundaries." She reached out and stroked Pad's neck. The horse moved into her touch.

"Darlin', you're family, and there aren't any boundaries."

Again, she smiled brightly and nodded. "No one wanted to come with us?"

He hadn't considered inviting the others, or that Reese might feel more comfortable having them around. "I'm sorry. I didn't invite anyone. I was being selfish and keeping you to myself. But if you'd feel more comfortable having someone here, I can fetch Rose or

Daisy. Basil is out in the pastures, fixing fences. He's pulling a trailer with an ATV."

Reese's eyes grew wide. "Can I ride that too?"

"You can ride anything you want. We've got tractors and motor-bikes and even a goat, but she won't be keen on having you on her back. That saying, stubborn as a goat, doesn't come from nowhere." He yanked on the saddle to make sure it was tight. If Sara was mad at him yesterday, just wait until she found out he'd been negligent and got Reese hurt from not securing her ride properly. He wanted to say, "Speaking of stubborn goats, how's your mother," but he didn't. Instead, he asked, "Have you talked to your mom today?" He helped her get her foot in the stirrup and boosted her onto Pad's back. As suspected, the horse stayed still the whole time.

While Reese shifted in the saddle to find a comfortable position, he mounted Titan and they set off toward the acreage he owned. Titan led and Pad followed. All Reese had to do was stay in the saddle, and the horse would do the rest.

"I had breakfast with her this morning. I left her to her pancakes and misery."

His heart lurched. Had he caused that unhappiness when he left last night? He'd been cordial and almost polite most of the night. But his emotions got in the way, and he hated how things ended. His parents had raised him better than that. Then he remembered her farewell. He owed her nothing. She'd wished awful things on him as he walked away. "I'm sorry to hear she's miserable."

They walked side by side. Pride filled him when she adjusted to the saddle and the bounce of the horse's gait so quickly. Many people tried to control the horse's movement, which was a losing battle. The best thing to do was move with the horse. The rider's bottom would appreciate it by the end of the ride.

"She somehow forgot she crashed her car and Bobby, the mechanic, told her it was totaled."

"Anyone could have seen that. The roof was crushed down on

one side. She is lucky she wasn't hurt worse." Thinking about finding her there pulled at his insides. He hated that he still cared, but he couldn't deny he did. "That must have scared her."

"Oh, you don't know my mom very well. During tornado season, she could go outside and shout at the wind, and it would turn in a different direction out of fear. Her distress comes not from the accident but from not being able to escape Aspen Cove." She played with the reins, making Pad move left and right. By the light in her eyes and the smile on her face, she was enjoying the experience.

"I'd hoped she'd stay longer." Hearing that Sara was dead set on leaving town gave him mixed emotions. On one hand, he wouldn't have to put up with her misplaced anger. On the other, a part of him wanted to find out about the woman she'd become.

"She came to get me, and now that she knows I won't go back to Oklahoma, there's no reason to stay. The problem now is she can't leave because not only is her car totaled, but she can't rent one for a few weeks. Having said that, she's a persistent person and will probably have a solution by the time we finish this ride. If she could, she'd order one online and have it delivered."

"I don't think Amazon sells cars."

"I'm sure you're right. That would be an interesting Prime delivery."

"You want to trot?"

She looked ahead at the pasture, then turned to him and nodded. "Sure, why not?"

He showed her how to raise herself in the saddle. "That's why the heel on boots is good. It gives you a grip."

They spent the next hour moving through the pastures and talking about the history of Aspen Cove.

"I can't believe I had all this in my family tree and didn't know about it."

The time that got wasted was almost criminal. "I'm sorry. I would have been there if I'd known you existed."

She reached over and held out her hand and he took it. "I believe that, but don't be too hard on my mother. I think, deep down inside, she's still just a girl trying to make someone proud. Too bad her parents didn't live long enough to see what she'd become. Don't get me wrong, she's a piece of work. But we are a product of our upbringing, and I think I turned out okay, so that means she must have been a pretty wonderful mom."

He thought about that for a minute. The woman holding his hand had turned out more than okay. She was an amazing gift to humankind. "I'll agree. Your mom did a great job raising you." The question in his mind was, had she done it alone? "You never had a father in your life?" She squeezed his hand, and let it go. The loss of her touch emptied him.

"No, I encouraged her to date, but she never did. There might have been a brief fling with someone at one of the vet conferences because a guy named Gordon called a lot one year, but she never brought a man to the house. I kind of feel guilty because I know I'm the biggest part of her life, and I left her. What's she going to do?"

"Live her life. That's all she can do, and you're not responsible for it." Doc's talk came back to him, and he pictured that napkin. Only now, it was Sara's, and all she had was her job because, like Doc said, kids don't belong to any of us. They are on loan.

"I know, but she was driving me crazy, and so I escaped to Aspen Cove. Uncle Frank was kind enough to let me stay at the house. I just needed time to find myself."

"And did you?" They rode back toward the stables.

"I found a lot more than myself. I found a boyfriend and a dad." She looked down. "What do I call you?"

That was a good question. "You call me what feels right to you, and I'll answer to it."

She lifted her head and gave him the sweetest smile. "I've never had a dad. I'd like to try it if it's not too weird."

They stopped in front of the stables, and he dismounted and

rounded her horse to help her down. "Honey, you always had a dad. We just didn't know it, and I'd love to hear that name on your lips."

She stood in front of him. "Thanks, Dad."

He pulled her into his arms and gave her a bear hug.

Lily ran out of the stables with a look of fear on her face. "Dad, something's really wrong with Hellion."

CHAPTER ELEVEN

"Okay, thank you." Sara set her phone on the table. For the last two hours, she'd sat there and tried to find any mode of transportation she could to get her back to Tulsa, but nothing was available. The closest thing she found to a vehicle was a Segway she could order through Amazon, or a mobility scooter she could rent from the medical supply store in Copper Creek. The first one would send her to the second on the first fall, and both needed charging after several miles.

"Cheer up. It isn't that bad." Maisey arrived to give Sara what seemed like her millionth refill. She held her jittery hand over her cup and shook her head. Another cup would put her over the edge. "It's pretty bad. I'm stuck here."

Maisey took the seat across from her. "As far as places to be stranded, this isn't the worst. You could be in a tent up in the hills. Imagine being in that hailstorm and unprotected."

"I was stupid to drive in it. Lloyd warned me, but I didn't listen. All I wanted was to run away."

Maisey reached for a cup, turned it over, and poured herself a coffee. "Running is okay as long as you know what you're running from. Murder hornets, mountain lions, and abusive husbands are good things to get away from. I fled here decades ago trying to escape the latter. What's got you on the move?"

Sara stared out the window. Several storefronts were now boarded over because the hail broke the glass. Cars sat unmoved with cracked windshields and pocked paint jobs. It was a real Armageddon out there.

"I thought I was avoiding conflict. I've had enough of that in my life, but as I sit here and look at the destruction before me, maybe I'm running from myself."

"What are you going to do about it?"

"I have little choice. I'm going to stay until I can go."

"Staying is good. Let me throw this out there. Did you ever think that maybe you've already done all the running you needed to do? Maybe without realizing, you ran here, and something, or someone, is keeping you here until you see what you need to see and do what you need to do. From what I know, Aspen Cove changed your life the last time you were here. Maybe it's time to change it again." She picked up her cup of coffee and the pot she used to fill it and shimmied out of the booth. "You need anything else before I go? Louise is taking over soon."

"No, I'm good."

"You are good. Don't let anyone tell you differently." Maisey walked off and disappeared through the swinging doors to the kitchen.

Sara opened her bag and took out enough money to pay her bill and leave a hefty tip. She'd taken the space for hours, and it was time to leave.

As soon as she walked outside, the sun washed her with warmth, and she had to admit it wasn't so bad being stuck here. The air smelled like pine and honeysuckle, which made her smile. In her day-to-day life, animals surrounded her so all she smelled was wet fur and dog farts. Yep, this wasn't too bad.

She didn't know what to do with herself for the rest of the day, so she took everything in. Seeing the bakery across the street had her lifting her nose into the air out of habit. Was it her imagination, or did she smell brownies? She was a sucker for gooey, warm brownies. Oh, who was she kidding? She was a sucker for any brownie.

She walked into B's Bakery and a bubbly blonde greeted her. "You must be Sara." The woman wiped her hands on her apron, walked around the counter, and stood in front of her.

Sara thought she would offer her a handshake, but she was yanked forward and wrapped in a hug. "I'm Katie. It's so nice to meet you. I just love your daughter. She's the best."

Those words made her stand taller. There was nothing like parental pride. "Thank you. She's an amazing human being." Saying it out loud fortified the statement. Not only because it was the truth, but because if Reese was amazing, she was confident it was because she wasn't too awful a parent. "Did I smell brownies?"

Katie let her go and rushed behind the counter. "That's my secret weapon to increase afternoon sales."

"It brought me in."

"The first treat is on the house." She wrapped a brownie in tissue and passed it across the counter.

"Thank you." Sara was filled to the gills with coffee, but had room for a treat. When she took a bite, all doubt was erased. Katie's brownies would be her drug of choice while in Aspen Cove. "I'll take a half-dozen more of these, please."

"Coming right up."

While Katie packaged her goodies, she took in the old bakery. A lot had changed, but much remained the same. It still had the same old floor and metal tables, but somehow was fresher and modernized. There were photos of the daily muffins interspersed with framed cross-stitch pictures on one wall. On the opposite side was something called a wishing wall.

"What's this?" She pointed to the corkboard filled with sticky notes.

Katie looked up and smiled. "That's my project. Trust me, it works. You fill out a sticky note and tell the wall what you want or need, and somehow it miraculously shows up."

"Wow." She walked over and picked up a sticky note and a pen. "Why not?" She took a seat and wrote *I need a c.*

"Just don't ask for a car. Nobody's going to see that wish come true. This town is generous, but we aren't miracle workers."

She almost tore her note up but made a game of it instead. "What starts with a C?" She figured she'd write whatever Katie said.

"Cowboy."

She finished the word and tacked her note to the board. It wasn't until she put it up there that the implication of that wish hit. "The last thing I need is a cowboy." She reached to pull it down, but Katie waved her hand to stop her.

"It's already up. Even if you take it down, the board knows what you wrote, and it will do its magic anyway."

"Hogwash. You and I know what I wrote, and I only wrote it because you said cowboy. It's more your wish than mine."

"Not true. I was just a vessel of inspiration. You threw out the thought, and I completed it."

Sara reached up and snagged the note off the board and tucked it into her back pocket. "I'm taking it back."

Katie slid the pink box across the counter. "You can try, but I'm fairly sure the powers that be are working on it already. I started that board years ago because I needed something positive to focus on, and honestly, it's taken on a life of its own."

"I'm giving it a little rest then." She paid for her treats. "It's a pleasure meeting you, Katie."

"You too, Sara." She pointed to the box. "I added a few extras so you can get addicted to more. I want to clean up the town square, and I finance those projects through the bakery."

Sara looked outside. "There's a town square?"

Katie shrugged. "Not really, but there's a little park on the lake side of town, and I thought a lovely pergola and a garden would be nice. Maybe a gigantic Christmas tree for a community tree lighting."

"You're ambitious."

"No, I'm grateful. This town gave me a life, and I will spend the rest of mine paying it forward."

The door opened, and in walked a handsome man carrying a pretty little girl. "Mama!" The little girl wiggled from the man's arms, and once she was on her feet, she ran to Katie.

"This is the life they gave me." She bent over and picked up the girl. "This is my daughter, Sahara, and that handsome hunk of man is my husband, Bowie."

Sara cocked her head. "Bowie Bishop?"

He nodded. "Do I know you?"

"No, but I know you. I'm Sara Arden, and I think I'm neighbors with your dad."

He chuckled. "You're behind in the news. My father is married to Maisey, and Katie and I and our little munchkin live in the beach house to your left. My brother and his wife, Sage, live to your right."

"Wow, it's a small world."

"Smaller than you realize," Katie said. "I'll tell you something about this man. He's only loved two women and one heart."

Sara looked at them in confusion. "I don't understand."

Katie shifted Sahara to her hip. "Here's the short version. Do you know who Brandy Bennett was?"

Sara nodded. "Yes, she hung out with Reese when my daughter was younger."

"Well, Bowie and Brandy were soulmates, but she passed in a car accident. I had a bad ticker and got her heart." She tapped her chest. "I came here because of a pink letter." She pointed to the frame on the opposite wall. "And I convinced this man that I was worth the risk of falling in love with the same heart twice." She pulled on Sahara's pigtail. "Then this little miracle was born, and so you see ... that wall works because all I wished for was a life, and I got the best one."

Bowie walked behind the counter and hugged Katie. While they were having their moment of family bliss, she walked out. That's

81

what she wanted, too. She had the dream of the house and white picket fence, and a half dozen kids, but no one ever listened to her wishes. She glanced down at the pink box. It wasn't a pink letter that would change her life, but those brownies would be delicious tonight on the deck with a sweet wine.

She crossed the street and walked into the veterinarian's office. If she was going to be here, she might as well make herself useful.

A bubbly receptionist said, "Welcome to chaos." The chairs were filled with people, and the woman behind the counter looked frazzled. "Do you have an emergency? As you can see, we're pretty filled up."

Sara glanced around and wasn't sure which were the pets and which were the owners. In one chair was an older woman carrying a cat wearing a superman onesie. Next to her was a little girl nearly strangling a poor pug.

"Bailey," the girl's mom said, "You're going to choke Cupcake to death."

Sara walked over and showed her how to cradle the pup. "She'll love you more if she's alive."

She looked at the rest, which included a parrot, a goat, and something that resembled a lizard, but it was in a cage, so she couldn't be sure.

Out of the back came a frayed young woman with a name tag that read Dr.

Charlie Whatley. "Who's next?"

Sara stepped forward. "I'm Sara Arden, and I'm a licensed vet in Tulsa. While I can't practice solely here, I can practice under your supervision. How can I help?"

"You can help?"

"I can. Do you want to check my credentials?"

"No, I know who you are. My father told me about you."

"Who's your father?"

"Dr. Parker. Do you prefer big animals or small ones?"

"I'll take the farm animals. Where can I get a jacket and a room?"

"Eden will show you the way." Charlie pointed to the kid with the lizard. "You're next."

Eden stood and led Sara toward the door.

Sara stopped and pointed at the goat. "You're with me."

Thirty minutes and two patients later, Eden said, "Dr. Whatley was wondering if you could take a ride to a nearby ranch and see about a horse?"

"I wish I could, but I don't have a car."

Eden smiled. "No problem. My husband, Thomas, has offered to drive. His truck was in the firehouse garage when all the hail came down. He's a neatnik, and I'm always teasing him because he spends at least an hour a week giving it some love, but outside of the police vehicles and a few others who were lucky, we're the only ride in town, so Thomas is like Aspen Cove's private taxi when he's not on duty."

It wasn't like she had anything else to do. "Does Dr. Whatley have a house call kit I can borrow?"

"Yes. Follow me." She led her to the front desk, where the bag sat waiting.

Dr. Whatley was on her haunches telling Bailey not to put beans in her dog's nose. When she rose, she pulled Sara in for a hug. "Thank you so much. I'm more of a domesticated animal caregiver and leave the farm animals to the vet in Copper Creek, but with the storm damage, no one has a way to get there." She put her card in Sara's hands. "I'm a phone call away."

"Thomas is here," Eden said and pointed to the black truck parked in front of the clinic. She picked up Sara's pink box of treats she'd left on the desk and handed them to her. "Thank you for helping."

Sara introduced herself to Thomas, and they got on the road. While legally she wasn't supposed to practice without a Colorado license, she looked up the law and found that she hadn't misrepresented herself and could practice under indirect supervision as long as Dr. Whatley asked her to. That was good enough in her book.

She checked her emails while Thomas drove to one of the outlying ranches. If her memory served her correctly there were several. When he stopped the truck, she looked up and found Lloyd and Reese standing there. Her breath caught in her throat. "No, it can't be."

CHAPTER TWELVE

"Where's Dr. Whatley?" Lloyd asked as Sara got out of the truck.

"Tending to a lizard with a skin condition." She pulled a bag from the back and walked toward him and Reese. "Hi, honey." She kissed her daughter on the cheek and turned to Lloyd. "Where's the patient?" She glanced back at Reese. "A little warning would have been nice."

Reese shrugged. "I didn't know you were coming. I offered to call you, and Dad said no, he'd call the vet in town."

"Why are you here?" Lloyd asked and pointed to the stables before walking that way.

"Yeah, Mom. Last I heard, you were planning grand theft auto to escape."

She stopped and turned around. "Hold on." Sara marched back to where Thomas stood by his truck. He and Reese followed. "Thank you for the ride. Can I give you gas money?" Lloyd liked that she thanked him and offered. It was a kind gesture, but he knew how it would end.

"No, ma'am. This is Aspen Cove, and we take care of our own."

Thomas pulled a business card from his pocket and offered it to Sara. "This is my contact information. Just call when you're ready to return."

She took the card and looked at it. "Thank you for your kindness." She glanced down at the pink box she had sitting atop the home visit kit. "What about a brownie?"

He smiled. "That I will take." She opened the box, and he took out a treat. "Don't forget to call when you need a ride."

"I will." She closed the box and settled it back on top of the kit.

"I'll take her back." Lloyd didn't mind returning Sara to the beach house. Only this time, he wouldn't insist they have a chat. Everything went well from the wine to the view, but the talk about what happened was where it went to hell in a handbasket.

"Are you going back to town now?" Reese asked Thomas.

"I am."

Reese turned to Lloyd. "I know I should unsaddle the horse and give her a brush down."

Lloyd waved his hand in the air. "It's okay, sweetie. We can take care of it. You get back to town. Let me know when you want to take another ride."

She threw herself into his arms and said, "Thanks, Dad. It was the best day I've had in a long time." She turned to Thomas. "I could use the ride you offered my mom."

The two of them got into the truck and took off, leaving him and Sara staring at each other.

She could have said a lot. He was certain she had questions like how he'd gone from Lloyd to Dad in a day, but she asked nothing except, "You want to tell me what's going on with the horse?"

He led her into the stables and into the stall where his daughter Lily stood next to Hellion.

"Dad, he's like stone." She put her hand on his flank, and Hellion stiffened, and then his muscles spasmed. A wave of ripples moved from Hellion's flank to his neck.

Sara pushed past him and stood by the horse. "Does he have a recent injury?"

Lloyd nodded. "Front right leg. I cleaned it and bandaged it."

Sara turned to Lily. "Do you drive?"

"Yes, I can."

"Good." She set the pink brownie box aside and opened the house call kit. Inside, she removed a needle and a syringe. Turning to him, she said, "I think your horse has tetanus. I'll draw a blood sample and have Lily take it to Dr. Whatley for confirmation."

"Tetanus? But isn't that deadly?" he asked.

She nodded. "Usually, but your horse hasn't met me, and I'm no quitter." She stood in Hellion's line of sight. "You're not a quitter either, are you, boy?"

She quickly drew the blood and handed it to Lily. "Take this to town and wait for Dr. Whatley to test it. I'll call ahead and tell her you're coming. She'll be sending some things back with you, so wait for them."

Lily held her hand out for Lloyd's keys and then raced out of the stables.

"You think it's tetanus?"

She walked around Hellion and pointed out his stiff posture and extended tail, the ears at attention, and his third lid, which was visible but sunken. "Those are telltale signs of the disease." She went to the sink, washed her hands, and then gathered things from kit she'd brought from Dr. Whatley's office. "Do you have a space in the barn where he can be alone? The less commotion, the better."

"Yes. Let me get it ready. Do you need me here?"

She moved back to the horse's side and donned a pair of gloves. "Nope, I don't need you." She took off her gloves, pulled out her phone, and dialed. When he heard her talking to Dr. Whatley, he hustled out of the stables.

Her words shouldn't have bothered him, but they did. He was a man who needed to be needed. Having Sara in town was messing

with his mind, or maybe it was all ego. Being needed was a funda-
mental constant in his life. It started from a young age when his
parents needed him to help with the ranch.

His life was based on need. The land required him to maintain it.
The equipment needed him to keep it running. His family needed
him for everything, or they used to, but even they needed him less.
The animals needed him to care for them, but it looked like he'd
failed Hellion.

If his horse died, he'd be broken. He'd spent almost as much time
with his horse as he had his wife. Poor Carol, she wasted away in
front of him, and he was powerless to help her. So, yes, it burned his
chaps for Sara to say she didn't need him. Of course, she did. Right
now, she needed him to get a place ready for Hellion, which meant
his horse needed him too.

He marched into the barn and shifted the equipment around to
make space for Hellion. Once he was finished laying down the hay,
he returned to the stables. He walked in and found her with her head
resting against the horse's neck, and she was talking to him.

He held back because this was a special moment, and he was
curious about what she would say.

"You're a good boy, aren't you?" She stroked his fur and hummed.
"You need to make it, okay, buddy? Your owner is already mad at me
for keeping his daughter away. Please don't die on him because I fear
he'll blame me. I'd be heartbroken if I disappointed him twice in one
visit."

He wouldn't blame her. He blamed himself. He was pretty good
at keeping up with vaccinations, but he couldn't remember if the
horses got their yearly booster. And if he couldn't recall, then it was
likely it didn't happen. He'd remedy that while she was here and ask
her to vaccinate all of them. He cleared his throat, so she'd know he
was there, and she jumped away from the horse.

"I've got the space ready," he said.

She nodded. "Take him slowly. His joints are stiff, and it's uncomfortable for him to walk. We'll need to make sure his water and food are high enough, so he won't have to move too much to get to it."

Lloyd hadn't thought of that, but he could rig the water trough and food to work for this situation. "Tell me what you need, and I'll make it happen. What do you need, Sara?"

CHAPTER THIRTEEN

What did she need? She needed a lot of things. However, he wasn't talking about her personally, but professionally.

"I'll get the bag, and you bring the horse."

As she walked toward the barn, many things she needed came to mind. Clarity about being back in Aspen Cove was one of them. As soon as she'd driven down Main Street, her sixteen-year-old inner teenager resurfaced. Something about this town made her feel youthful and relevant, like she mattered. Maybe it was because she was allowed to be herself again.

All these years, she'd been watching herself through someone else's lens. At first, it was her parents', whom she disappointed. Even after they passed, she tried to please them. And instead of being her own person, she turned into the doppelgänger of her mother—the buttoned-down fun-sucker of the family.

Reese never met Sara the woman, she only got to see the authoritarian, which was just another way of describing a fun-sucker. All her life, she wanted to please someone, and in the end, she hadn't satisfied a single soul.

She finished vet school and opened a practice. Even though her parents weren't happy that she pursued veterinary medicine, hopefully they would see that she had found success in her field. Sadly, there was no way to know.

"What else do you need?"

She shook herself free of her thoughts. "I need you to trust me."

"I do. Look around you. I don't have anyone else to lean on when it comes to Hellion. You're all we got, so we have to trust you."

She hated that his trust came out of necessity and wasn't given freely. They walked side by side at a slow pace for the horse. "I cleaned the wound again. You did a good job, but the bacteria must have been deep. Tetanus is anaerobic, which means it doesn't need oxygen to thrive." She didn't know why she was giving him the down and dirty details. Maybe she wanted him to value her education. Perhaps it was her way of proving she was qualified. She'd finished school and started a veterinarian practice while raising their child alone. She could see all the wrong turns she'd made, and if she could go back in time, she would have done it differently. "I'm sorry for all the pain I've caused."

He led Hellion into his new space and turned to Sara. "It was more of a shock than pain, Sara. I can't fixate on the years I didn't have with her. All I can focus on is the years I do. The one thing I learned from Carol's death was that life is short. Don't put off what you want to do today until tomorrow because it might not come."

"Do you mean that?" Could she tap into her inner sixteen-year-old and borrow some recklessness? From the first time she saw him again in the diner she wondered one thing: Was he still an amazing kisser?

"I do."

He was right about one thing. She couldn't put this off another minute. She set the medical kit down in front of him and stood on top of it. Lloyd was over six feet tall, and the extra six inches the case gave her put her eye to eye with him. "I've tucked my responsible adult self away for a few minutes, and I'm letting my inner child rule right now. In my head, you were the best kisser ever, and I need to know if that was true or if my younger self didn't have enough experience to make that judgment."

He chuckled. "Are you asking me to kiss you?"

Embarrassment heated her cheeks. She shifted her weight and nearly fell off the box but plunged into his chest instead of falling backward. "Never mind." Her hands splayed across the hard muscles under his plaid shirt. For a man in his fifties, he was in great shape. She imagined it was all that time on the range that kept him honed and toned.

His hands covered hers. "You thought I was a good kisser?"

"I had little to go on. You were the second boy I'd kissed."

His eyes narrowed. "Who was the first?"

"Barry Schenkel in a game of spin the bottle. He wanted to kiss my friend Tara, but the bottle landed on me. It was a total disappointment for both of us." She tried to pull away, but he closed his hands over hers and held her there.

"Don't run again, Sara." He let go of one hand, so he was free to cup her cheek. "That young girl I made love to turned into a beautiful woman."

He leaned forward, and she held her breath. Just as his lips neared hers, Lily walked inside the barn. "I'm back."

Sara's heart thundered in her chest. She jumped down, grabbed the box, and hurried toward the horse.

Lily looked at both of them like she was putting a puzzle together. "I got the things you needed." She held out an envelope. "Dr. Whatley said the test results are inside."

Sara opened the envelope and frowned.

"Is it bad?" Lily asked.

Lloyd went to his daughter and wrapped his arm around her shoulder. "He probably has tetanus."

"Oh, my goodness. Will he die?"

Lloyd looked at Sara, who said, "I'll do everything I can to save him. Did Dr. Whatley have the medications I asked for?"

"They're right here." Lily lifted another case that looked like the twin of the one she had brought along. "Did I catch you two in a kiss?"

Sara took the kit and headed toward Hellion. "Don't be ridiculous. I had something in my eye."

Lily laughed. "Oh, the 'something in my eye' routine. I tried that one with a teacher. It never works unless your eyes are red and swollen. Good try, though." She turned to her father. "None of us mind if you date, Dad. It's been years, and you know what mom would have said."

"You've got horses to tend to, young lady, so mind that business instead of mine. I removed the saddles from Pad and Titan, but they need a good grooming. That should keep you out of our hair for a while."

Lily pointed to the hayloft. "Should I text before I come in next time? I'd hate to find you rolling in the hay." She turned to look at Sara. "It's a great place to hide, and ... you know what I mean."

Lloyd pointed to the door. "Out, young lady, or I might turn you over my knee."

Lily turned to walk away but stopped. "Don't let him scare you. His bark is far worse than his bite. I can't remember once in my lifetime that I've met his belt. None of the kids have. But he has a look that will make us turn tail and run." She jutted her chin toward Lloyd. "Yep, that's the one. See you two lovebirds soon."

Lily left, and Sara went straight to the horse. She gave him a vaccination to help boost his immune system and then a neurotoxin to eat at the active bacteria. She followed up with a dose of heavy antibiotics.

"Now we wait and see."

"What are his odds?" Lloyd asked.

She shrugged. "Statistically, not great, but conservatively, I'd say 50/50. Do you have a cot I can use?"

"Why would you need a cot?"

She'd given this scenario a great deal of thought. If she left the horse and he died, she'd feel responsible, so she'd spend every minute she could with the beast until he was out of the woods or succumbed.

"I'm staying with him."

"No, you're not."

"Oh, yes, I am." She gathered up her supplies. "I'm not leaving him. Let's immunize the others, so there isn't an epidemic on the Big D ranch." She laughed at the name. "Speaking of the ranch, who in their right mind would name it Big D?"

"We owe that to the first settlers." He let his head hang. Was it to hide the blush that crept to the tips of his ears?

"I bet you caught a lot of hell from that name."

He took the case from her hands. "I didn't. My generation wasn't bold enough to think of Big D as anything but my John Wayne-like great-grandfather. Angus Dawson was close to six-foot six-inches tall. He caught hell for being a cattle rancher and having the name Angus. Basil caught a lot of hell for coming from a ranch called the Big D. I'd say he got a lot of action, too. You know, curious minds wanted to know."

Her eyes lowered. "Well, if that endowment runs in the family ..." She blushed like a schoolgirl. "He made a lot of curious women happy." They moved toward the stables. "They don't say hung like a horse for nothing." She slapped her hand over her mouth. "Sorry, that was unexpected and unfiltered."

"How long have you kept reckless Sara bottled up?"

They moved past Lily, who was brushing down Pad, and walked into the stables. "Since that summer. Reckless isn't a good look on me."

"I'd disagree." Lloyd glanced around and pulled her into his arms. "I fell in love with reckless Sara. It's good to see her back." He pressed his lips to hers. It was a short, almost chaste kiss, but inside her body, it was NC-17 all the way. Those emotions from way back when burst free, and all Sara wanted to do was climb him like a tree. But when she heard the stable door creak, she jumped back.

"I'll just be a minute," Lily said. "Pretend I'm not here."

Sara was mortified once again. She could plausibly deny the kiss the first time because it hadn't happened, but she was caught in the act this time.

CHAPTER FOURTEEN

"What's the verdict?" Lloyd watched Sara prepare the vaccines for the other horses. Every member of his family had a horse, and there were a few boarders, so the stalls were full.

"What are we talking about?" She started at the first stall to immunize the horses against tetanus but pointed to the other stalls. "Are these all yours?"

"Nope, but I have the authority to allow vet care, so do your thing." He opened one of the gates. "This is Rose's horse, Bud."

"I see a trend here. Rose Bud, Lily Pad."

"They were little girls when they named them, and they thought they were clever."

Moving to the stall next to Bud, he said, "Daisy's horse is named Chain."

Sara chuckled. "I can't say I would have come up with anything cleverer. I always thought I'd have a horse named Juniper."

Lloyd laughed. "You'd get along fine with the girls."

They moved from stall to stall. "What goes with Violet?" she asked.

He watched her inject the vaccine into Bloom's neck. "Not much, so she chose Bloom. The next horse is Field."

"Must be Poppy's."

"Being the oldest, she tried to come up with an ingenious name association and wanted to name her horse Opium, but Carol put a kibosh on that."

"And you were okay with it?"

"Naming a horse is like naming a child. It's personal, and I think all names should be considered. Opium would have been a good name for Field as she's high-strung and unpredictable."

"Names are hard, but I think people grow into them. None of us look like our name when we're born. I'm certain my mother didn't look at me and say, 'That kid looks like a Sara.'"

"How did you come up with Reese?"

She moved to the last horse and gave it a shot. "Witherspoon. I'd watched several of her movies and liked her as an actress. She's an activist and advocate for women's rights. I wanted my daughter—"

"Our daughter," he corrected.

"Yes, I wanted our daughter to grow up to be a strong, independent woman. I wanted her to have a mind of her own, but then the accident happened."

"She seems all the things you wanted her to be. She's got a mind of her own."

"That's a recent addition. One day she packed up her car and said she was coming to Aspen Cove." She left the stall and returned to the table where she'd set out the meds. "I'm sure she was rebelling. In hindsight, I was controlling. There's so much guilt with parenting. You do your best, but sometimes your best isn't good enough."

"She's a remarkable woman, Sara. You must be incredibly proud of her."

She tucked all the needles in a disposable sharps container and packed the vaccine vial away. "I am. Her career wouldn't have been what I chose for her, but she does well. It's challenging to make a living as a writer, and she's found her way despite the obstacles."

"Speaking of careers, why did you become a veterinarian?"

She grinned. "I did it to make my parents mad."

"Aww, so that rebel you locked inside was still rearing her head occasionally."

"They wanted me to be a doctor or a lawyer, but I chose animals because they're easier to get along with than people." She closed the kit and set it aside. "Besides, I wasn't allowed to have animals when I was growing up, so by going into veterinary sciences, it was my way of having every animal I could for a time."

"What's your favorite?"

She smiled and shook her head. "You'll laugh at me."

"I promise I won't laugh, and if I feel the need, I'll turn my back, so you won't see me."

"How chivalrous of you." She stared at him for a long second. "I love mini-pigs and goats."

He remained quiet for as long as he could, then turned his back and laughed. "They serve no purpose."

"Why does everything need to have a purpose? Maybe their purpose is simply to bring a smile to my face."

"If you want a small animal, then get chickens. At least they lay eggs."

A gurgling growl escaped. "You are so typical of most men."

"No, I'm practical. All they do is eat and poop. They produce nothing of value. Where's the payoff?"

"Does everything have to have one?"

He spread his arms. "This is a working ranch. Everything and everyone here earns its keep. Everything except the goat, Sadie. Poppy wanted to make goat cheese and Carol said it was okay. Sadie never produced a drop of milk because Sadie is a he. He isn't earning his keep."

"I'm earning my keep by trying to save your horse."

"Exactly, you were hired to come here to tend to Hellion. I'll pay your fee."

"Fine, but do you kiss all the vets who come here to vaccinate your beasts?" She picked up her case and walked toward the door.

"Only the ones who ask for it." He had a long stride but had to walk double-time to keep up with her half jog, half run.

"That was a mistake. I won't be asking for more kisses from the boss. It's bad to mix business with pleasure."

"Now we're back to the beginning of the conversation."

"What do you mean?" she asked.

"My kissing skills were in question. What's the verdict?"

"I don't kiss and tell." She entered the barn and walked toward Hellion.

"Not true. You said Barry Schenkel was an awful kisser."

"I did not. I said the kiss was a disappointment."

He grabbed a nearby hammer, pulled a few nails from a drawer, and secured the hay net and water to the wall so Hellion didn't have to bend to reach them.

"Which is a nice way to say the kiss sucked. I'm asking if my kiss was better than Barry Schenkel's?"

She turned and smiled at him. "That's like comparing apples to oranges. Barry Schenkel was fourteen, but at his age, there was potential."

"And at my age?"

She pulled over a folding chair she found leaning against the wall and sat. "You've got potential too." She looked around the barn. "Can I get a cot, please?"

"You're not sleeping in the barn."

"Yes, I am. I'm not leaving your horse alone." She got up, went to the pink bakery box she'd left behind, and pulled out a brownie. "I've got my phone and brownies. What more could I want?"

He leaned against a wooden post. "A change of clothes? Something to drink? More kisses?"

She made a *pfft* sound and plopped herself back into the chair. "Those kisses are what got me into trouble in the first place."

"Okay, so no more kisses. In case you were wondering ... you still kiss like a sixteen-year-old."

She gasped. "How rude."

He loved the way her cheeks turned pink. "Rude wasn't my intention. You have the spirit of a teen still living inside you. Sadly, young Sara had to grow up too fast, and she didn't get to live out her teens like she was supposed to."

"Tell me about it. There was no homecoming and no prom for me. I was breastfeeding while everyone was going to Europe for summer break." She grabbed her breasts, which, of course, made him look at them. They were a perfect handful. "I went from pleasant and perky to soft and saggy overnight." She touched her tummy. "Babies do crazy things to a body. I used to have abs, but now I have flabs."

He pushed off the wooden post and stood in front of her. "You have the body of a warrior and should wear your scars like badges of honor. They tell a story of where you've been and what you've done. Sometimes the tale is funny, sometimes sad, but it's always interesting. I hope you'll stay long enough to tell me your story, Sara."

CHAPTER FIFTEEN

"There's not much to tell. Honestly, I'd hate to bore you to death." She rose from the chair and walked to the horse. He was still stiff and uncomfortable, but knowing she'd done all she could for him made him somehow look better. "Tell me about Hellion."

He moved to stand beside her. "He comes by his name honestly. I was at a horse auction to get Poppy a new horse and he was there. He refused to let anyone touch him. At the end of the auction, I heard the owner talking about putting him down. What good was he if he couldn't sell or ride him?" A look of sadness briefly crossed his face before he continued.

"Since I wasn't there for me, I hadn't inspected the stallion, but I imagined the fact that he was a stallion played a big part in his attitude. Testosterone creates a lot of drama in man and beast."

"So, you bought him?" Looking at the gruff-looking man Lloyd had matured into, she wouldn't have taken him for the softhearted sap she saw now.

He turned his head toward the horse as if in slow motion. "I did." He nodded and spoke slowly. "It tore me up because he wasn't a bad horse. He was simply misunderstood. As a man, it's normal to have unchecked energy coursing through my body." He chuckled. "Men aren't much different from horses. Hell, we're simple creatures." Reaching out, he gently touched Hellion with the softest hand, as if he were afraid to hurt him. "He was bursting at the seams. I brought home Field and Hellion that day." He pulled his shirt up to show a jagged scar.

"What the hell happened to you?" She leaned forward to skim the scar with her fingers, but he let his shirt drop.

"It wasn't like I brought him home and he behaved. I tried to break him, but he broke me a few times before we had an agreement." He pointed toward the stables. "I had this idea that if he got it out of his system, he'd calm down. So, I bred him with Field, and they had Bud and Pad. When it became clear that Hellion was a stallion through and through, I gelded him. It broke my heart, but he calmed down."

"I hear marriage and children are the equivalents of gelding for a man." Lots of men cheated because they had the energy and mindset of a stallion, but Lloyd didn't seem the type.

He laughed. "I guess for some. I think it's important to pick the right person. I got lucky. Carol and I were well-matched. She loved the land as much as I did."

She didn't want to pry into his life, but she was curious about it. "How did she die?"

He smiled. "On her terms. Carol had ALS, and it took everything from her but her spirit. She was a force to be reckoned with. In a lot of ways, she was like Hellion. She lived every day to the fullest." He moved around his horse as if inspecting him. "It started with numbness and tingling and progressed until her lungs seized, but she got the last word in."

She could see that it pained him to talk about his wife, but she could also see that he did so with pride.

"You don't have to talk about it if it's too hard on you."

He shook his head and walked away from the horse. "No, it's a good thing. Talking about her keeps her memory alive." He shut the gate to the makeshift stable and nodded toward the barn door. "How about a little walk?"

She didn't want to leave the horse alone. If she insisted on staying in the barn, Lloyd would leave her to her madness, but she wasn't ready to let him go, either. "A short walk would be great."

He laid his arm over her shoulder and led her into the sunshine. "I almost lost the ranch."

That took her by surprise. Lloyd was a practical man, and she couldn't see him being careless. "What happened?"

He started toward the stables, but as soon as Lily came into view, he pivoted and walked in the opposite direction. "Poppy's husband's father used to be my foreman, and he robbed me blind. For a good twenty years, I was a bitter, angry man. I owned a ranch that barely made ends meet. I had a wife who put on a brave face but died a little every day. I took my anger out on everyone."

A chill raced through her, and she shrugged off his arm. "What does that mean? Took your anger out."

He cupped her shoulder and pulled her closer to him. "I'm not that kind of man. When I said I took it out on everyone, I mean I was untrusting and unforgiving—a tyrant. Poor Poppy almost didn't get to marry Mark because I held a grudge against his father. I figured the apple didn't fall far from the tree."

She relaxed into his side as they walked through the pasture below the house. "Mark seems like a lovely young man, and Poppy seems so happy."

"She is, but she was miserable until Mark was allowed in her life, and that was all Carol's doing. She reminded me we aren't our parents, and we all have a choice in who we love. Just the other night, Doc reminded me that our kids aren't truly ours. They are only on loan to us for a short time. That's a tough pill to swallow when you think everything you've done is for their benefit."

"You don't think it was?"

He stopped, dropped his hand from her shoulder, and stepped over a rut in the ground before helping her cross it. She liked that he looked out for her. She'd never had anyone look out for her—ever. An odd sensation ribboned up her spine and sat warm and comfortable around her heart. She hated to admit it, but she still liked Lloyd. More than liked him. If she wasn't careful, he could break her heart again.

"I could puff out my chest and say yes, but I can see now that everything I've done has been for my benefit. I figured if I ran every boy off at the beginning, I saved them from heartache, but really, I was saving myself. Having five daughters isn't easy."

She thought about Reese. "Having one is no walk in the park, either. Don't let her quiet demeanor fool you. There's a hellion in our daughter, too." It was getting easier to refer to her as theirs. Selfishly, she wanted to keep Reese to herself, but her logical brain told her that Reese didn't belong to her. Lloyd was right, children grew up to be adults, and every adult had to make decisions. "Can I confess something?"

He stopped when they were knee deep in wildflowers. "I'm no priest, but I can't imagine there being a better place to cleanse your soul." He bent over and picked several blooms and handed them to her.

She brought them to her nose, but all she smelled was earth, sunshine, and a touch of his cologne sitting on the surrounding air.

"I came here fully intent on bringing Reese back, but when I got here, my daughter had blossomed into this confident woman. I tried to bully her into going back. I told her it was best for her, but that wasn't true. Her coming back was best for me. With Reese gone, I don't know who I am anymore."

He led her down a hill where several trees surrounded a small pond. "You're exactly who you were before, but now you have the freedom to be human, too."

"Oh, I'm human, all right." She thought about being superhuman and how that bubble burst the minute the woman at the car rental agency told her that her money wasn't any more special than the guy who called a minute before. There weren't any cars. "As proven because I can't summon a ride back to Tulsa."

"Is it imperative that you get back there right away? Will your business fail if you're gone for a time?"

She wanted to say yes, but it would be a lie. "My business thrives when I'm away. I think my staff likes my absence because I'm a fun-sucker."

He cocked his head and stared at her like she'd spoken a foreign language. "You're a what?"

"No one will miss me. If there's an ounce of fun happening near me, I ruin it with my practicality."

"Says the woman who loves pygmy goats and potbellied pigs." He folded his legs until seated at the pond's edge and patted the ground beside him. "Sit with me. We don't do this very often."

"Do what?" She sat beside him and plucked the petal from one daisy in her hand. She used a he-loves-me, he-loves-me-not mantra in her head, but the words were I'm-a-fun-sucker, I'm-not-a-fun-sucker.

"Just be. Look around and watch the grass grow. While we're living, life gets away from us, doesn't it?"

She watched a bird swoop down and dip into the still water to pluck a bug from the surface. "I bet that bug was just floating there watching the grass grow, and now he's lunch." She tossed the plucked petals from her hand to the side.

"Does he love you?" Lloyd asked.

She looked down at the discarded parts. "There is no he. I was doing a fun-sucker version, and according to that wise daisy, I'm not a fun-sucker, but I still kiss like a sixteen-year-old."

"That was a compliment. You kiss with the enthusiasm of a teenager, which is a good thing."

She let that soak in. "Oh, I thought you meant the inexperience of a young girl."

He leaned forward until his lips were almost touching hers. "I think I need to have another kiss just to make sure." He kissed her, only this time it wasn't chaste. This was pure lust mixed with sunshine and happiness. When he pulled back, he licked his lips like he was savoring her taste on them. "Definitely not the kiss of a teen. That there was all hot-blooded woman."

CHAPTER SIXTEEN

Nothing good ever came from Lloyd Dawson, or that was what she tried to tell herself, but it was a big fat lie. Reese came from him, and she was good. Those kisses were pretty awesome, too, but she couldn't let herself get wrapped up in him.

Turning her head back to the sky, she said, "Tell me more about your life here."

He leaned back on his elbows. "It's a simple life. I raise cattle and sell them off at auction. Jimmy, who is my current foreman, is at an auction now, but he should return today."

She laid back and let the tall grass act as a pillow. "What does a cow go for at auction?"

"It depends on the cow and the weight. I sell and buy mine in lots, which means I move a lot of cattle at one time. A trip to auction can cost or bring in thousands. Today is a bring-in-money day. It's later in the season for us, but they still sell."

Her lips still tingled. "Why did you kiss me again?"

He rolled to his side. "You were questioning your skill level, and I wanted to assure you that your kisses were just as sweet as I remembered them."

Up she popped. "I wasn't questioning the kiss. You wanted a rating."

He pushed himself to a sitting position. "I recall you said I could do better."

She shook her head. "No, I said you had potential." There was one thing Sara had, and that was perfect recall. In her line of work, there was no room for error. She wouldn't say she had a photographic memory, but she could recall almost anything that happened within hours or days. After that, she let it go, and things got a little fuzzy.

He stood and wiped the dirt from his jeans. "Potential in my book means not up to par. I hate failing, so trust me when I say I'll be upping my kissing game."

"Am I the first woman you've kissed since your wife passed?"

He offered her his hand and pulled her to her feet. "Nope. I kissed Elsa Buchanan." He rocked his head back and forth. "That's not exactly true." He shrugged and moved through the tall grass back toward the barn. "She kissed me."

"Are you claiming to be an innocent bystander?" She wanted to laugh because Lloyd didn't play the part of the unwilling victim well.

"Yep, she stood in front of me, gripped my neck, and yanked me down for a kiss."

She wasn't sure what to think about that. Lloyd was a good-looking man, and it didn't surprise her that other women wanted to kiss him. They weren't a couple, and she wanted to kiss him. Thinking about another woman's lips on his sent a surge of jealousy zipping through her. As fast as that feeling consumed her, she pushed it aside. There was nothing for her in Aspen Cove. Her life was in Tulsa, and it would serve her well to remember that.

"You poor helpless man. How did you fight her off?" She pulled up her hands and did her best impression of a boxer, jabbing left and right before she ended it with an uppercut.

"You tease, but I didn't ask for it."

"But you enjoyed it, right?"

His neck bloomed red, and the color rose to his ears. "It had been a long time since I'd been kissed."

She crossed her arms and trudged through the tall growth. "I'll take that as an affirmation of your enjoyment."

"It's not like you haven't kissed anyone. Reese told me there was some guy named Jordan."

"His name is Gordon, and I kissed him, but it wasn't good. He was like a jowly slobbering hound dog. No one wants a wet kiss like that."

"Why don't you date?" He stopped at the place where he helped her before, but she took a running start and crossed the crevice by herself. She didn't trust herself to not be an Elsa Buchanan and tug him down for another kiss if he touched her. Lack of affection was like starvation. Once you had a little taste of something, you wanted more. Lloyd gave her a sample of what she was missing. He was a single scoop of rocky road ice cream, but she needed a double scoop in a waffle cone with sprinkles, whipped topping and extra nuts.

"I've been busy raising our daughter."

"Oh, we're back to that. I think she's raised, and you did a fine job of it. Now it's time for you."

"The problem with that theory is that we assume because our kids are grown up, they won't need us anymore, but no matter how old they get, we will always be their parents so the concept of 'me time' is moot."

"You and I aren't all that different in how we think. The only difference is I've seen how brief life can be. I've loved, and I've lost."

She stopped and fisted her hands on her hips. "Don't you think I've lost too? My parents are gone. Losing you was like a death to me as well."

He tugged her into his arms and held her. "That summer was a blur. We met and fell in love, and then your parents were coming for the weekend, and I thought that was a good thing. I met them briefly and then you disappeared. It was a death for me, too."

"Did Carol know about me?"

"Yes, she always thought I should look you up and see what happened."

"Why didn't you?"

He gripped her shoulders and stepped back. "I feared those feelings would surface when I looked at you. I was happy with my life. There was no reason to borrow trouble."

"But you did see me."

He nodded. "Yes, and I was right to stay away because all those feelings flooded back. You'd been gone for years, but it was like only seconds had passed. That day on the beach when you ran toward me … I still loved you, but I couldn't, and wouldn't, do anything about it. I'm a man bound by honor. I was married and expecting a child. Carol and I were good together. I loved her. She was my rock and my best friend. After you left, she became my everything, but a part of my heart would always love you. You never forget your first true love."

She staggered back with the realization that he loved her. At least he did all those years ago.

"We aren't the same people we were back then."

He reached for her and brushed the hair away from her face. "Nope, we aren't. We're older, and wiser, and we know what we lost, and what we can gain."

"Are you saying you want to date me while I'm in town?"

He smiled, and though his eyes were crinkled at the corners, the young man he was all those years ago was still present.

"It wouldn't be unheard of to have a meal together."

She laughed. "I hear the date usually comes before the kiss."

"In this day and age, I'm not all that certain. The young ones have strange rules these days."

"I know. Our daughter picked up a hitchhiker and moved in with him the following week."

"I really should have a talk with that boy."

She laughed so hard she had to bend over and grab her belly. "I don't think that would go over well. You don't get to swoop in and make new rules for her."

"Did you have any rules at all? What happened to don't talk to strangers?"

"She learned that in kindergarten. If you hear her tell the tale, her car drove itself to where he stood. If you listen to Brandon, he was certain she was going to run him over."

They walked to the barn, where a man stood by the enormous doors. He waved his hand and smiled. "Howdy."

Lloyd nodded and said, "That's Jimmy." As they approached, Lloyd pointed to her. "This is Sara. She's a veterinarian who's taking care of Hellion. He's got tetanus."

"No shit? Must have gotten it that day when it hailed. That was a nasty gash." Jimmy tipped his hat. "Nice to meet you, ma'am." He looked at her and then at Lloyd. "Anything she needs, I'm here to help."

Lloyd frowned. "Your help isn't needed."

Jimmy's eyes grew wide. "Duly noted."

While flattering, she would not be a bone that two dogs fought over. "Not true. I need a cot and a sleeping bag. I plan to stay with the horse until he's out of the woods or worse case, I need to..." She was going to say put him down, but looked at Lloyd, whose eyes clouded over. "Well, let's hope for the best."

Jimmy stood there with a look of concern. "I'm a little confused. Should I get her a cot and a bedroll, or not?"

She said yes as Lloyd said no.

"You two figure it out. I'm too old to play these games." Jimmy tipped his hat and walked away.

"You hungry?" Lloyd asked. "I got a loaf of bread in the cupboard and a can of some kind of meat on the counter."

"You really know how to romance a girl."

"It's brand name canned meat," he said with a smile.

"Just so you know, if you're expecting a kiss, I want cloth napkins, candles, and wine."

"What kind of wine goes with deviled ham?"

They enjoyed a quiet lunch together in the barn. It wasn't fancy, and it wasn't a date.

CHAPTER SEVENTEEN

"Are you going to let her sleep in the barn?" Rose asked while setting the table for dinner.

Lloyd pinched the bridge of his nose. This wasn't a conversation he wanted to have with his kids. Talking about another woman was awkward, but he couldn't stay silent. "She's a stubborn woman like your mother, and no matter what logic I present, she's determined to stay with the horse."

"I caught them kissing," Lily said as she dumped a bag of salad into a bowl. His kids went silent and turned to look at him.

"What have we taught you about telling tales, young lady?" He shook his head and walked past her to the refrigerator to grab a beer. He popped the tab and leaned against the kitchen counter.

"A tale is an untruth," Violet said. "Is she telling the truth or not?"

As his children looked at him, he understood how intimidating a parent could be. Though he was their father, all of his kids looked at him with parental judgment.

"We kissed, and it was nice." He kicked off the counter and walked into the living room.

Basil let out a whoop that shook the windows. "Way to go, Dad. If you play your cards right, she could be in your bed by the end of the week."

"Hey, I won't have you disrespecting Sara. She's not that kind of woman." At least she didn't seem to be. "I've taught you better than that. Tomorrow you'll muck the stalls at five instead of six and don't forget Hellion in the barn."

His sisters snickered while Basil groaned. "That's an awful time."

"You're right. Four should suit you better."

When Basil opened his mouth, Lloyd held up his hand. "You want to make it three?"

"Dinner's ready. Should I get Sara?" Rose asked.

He looked out the window toward the barn. "I don't think she'll come. She says she's not leaving the horse." He turned to face his family.

"Well, she needs to eat." Rose put a serving of pasta on a plate. "How about I fix two plates, and you eat with her in the barn?"

That sounded nice and all, but he was pretty sure Sara had already had her fill of him. Earlier that day, he made them deviled ham sandwiches, and they sat in the barn and ate while she talked about veterinary school and living in Tulsa. The best thing Tulsa had going for it was Sara.

They'd sat staring at the barn walls when they were all talked out. He wanted to kiss her again, but she'd set the standard. She wanted wine, cloth napkins, and candles.

"I think we've had enough of each other for the night. Can one of you bring her dinner?"

Basil jumped in the air. "I'll do it. Fix two plates, and I'll join her. The longer I stay here, the earlier my shift gets."

Rose tossed a towel at his head. "I'll join her." She piled hot pasta and meat sauce on another plate and added a side salad and garlic bread to each. She walked to the door and turned to her siblings. "I'll get all the goods on Dad and report back later."

He flew from his chair. "Hold up. I'll take her the meal." He stared down at the tray. If he added cloth napkins, a candle, and a bottle of wine, would it make this a date? It was a thought, but he was sure they didn't have any of those things. The sweet stuff the girls loved that cost three bucks a bottle didn't count as wine.

He glanced past his kids to the wall of photos and his favorite of Carol in the wildflower field. She was right. They needed upgrades, and the first one he needed was his attitude about what was worthwhile and what wasn't. Had Carol wanted cloth napkins too? She never asked for them, but that didn't mean she didn't want them. He had no idea what women wanted these days.

Not true. He knew exactly what Sara wanted.

"Behave yourselves." Lloyd walked out the door and down the hill to the barn. When he stepped inside, he found Sara sitting on the edge of her cot—one he borrowed from Jimmy. She was talking on the phone. As a rancher, he had little use for cots. If the ground was good enough for his cattle, it was good enough for him. Besides, Lily was right. A sprinkling of hay worked well too. He didn't want to think about how she figured that part out. There were some things fathers didn't need to know.

"I brought dinner," he said, lifting the tray to show her. The only light was from the tack room behind her, and it cast an ethereal glow around her.

"Honey, I have to go. Your dad's here." She made a kissing sound into the phone and hung up. She stared as he neared. "You brought me dinner? I was going to have another brownie."

"You need sustenance, not sugar." He nodded toward the space beside her. "Care if I join you?"

She scooted over to make room for him. "I'll have you know there's milk and butter in there and flour, so that covers dairy and grain."

He sat beside her and looked at the tray in his lap. "I can't say it will be good, but it'll be edible, and there are vegetables."

"Meat sauce is my favorite. Who made this?"

He handed her a plate and fork. "Rose and Ragu. My girls aren't known for their culinary skills."

She spun her fork in the pasta and took a bite. He wanted to wipe the tiny bit of sauce left behind on her lip, but she flicked out her tongue to lick it clean. When did a simple action like that become so sexy? It was the moment she returned, and he realized he wasn't immune to her kisses. She may lack experience, which was hard for him to believe, but everything about Sara came with a level of enthusiasm that was intriguing.

"It's decent. I can't say I'm a Bobby Flay or Martha Stewart in the kitchen, but these days, women have more to offer than a good meal and a clean house."

"I agree. As for my girls, they are far from Suzy Homemaker. They bring excellent horse skills to the table, and they aren't afraid of anything." He considered that for a second. "That's not true. Rose hates spiders, and Daisy isn't a fan of snakes."

"In my line of work, you can't be afraid of much of anything."

"What's the strangest animal you've ever worked on?"

"A human gunshot victim."

He nearly dropped his plate. "What?"

She shrugged and took a bite of salad, and after she swallowed, she continued. "There was a robbery down the street, and an officer was shot. The hospital was too far, and an ambulance wouldn't arrive for a while, so his partner carried him into my office, and I provided triage."

"You didn't lie when you said you were a doctor."

She laughed. "I'm not supposed to work on humans, but I wasn't going to let him die."

"Did he live?"

She frowned and sighed. "Nope, I killed him with my lack of experience, but you win some and lose some."

He stared at her in disbelief until she laughed. "Just kidding. He lived and is one of my best customers. He's one of the nicest, anyway. He's got a shepherd named Zeus, and a dachshund named Medusa."

"Fascinating. Do you have animals now?"

She took a bite of bread, and a stream of melted butter ran down her chin until he swiped it up and licked his finger.

"That was mine."

He lifted his eyes in a challenge. "Come and get it."

She shifted on the cot, and for a second, he thought she'd put her plate down and climb into his lap, but she didn't. She took another bite and licked the melted butter from her lips in a seductive way that made him aware she was teasing him.

"I used to have Z." She shook her head. "That's not true. Z has always belonged to Reese. He allows me to pet him occasionally. I have a beta fish in the office named Betta White, but he won't live to be ninety-nine like the Golden Girl. At three, he's in his golden years."

"Reese has a dog?" He thought he'd already learned so much about her, but he had no idea she had a pet. "She didn't tell me."

"You've had little alone time with her. She has a lot to tell, but an afternoon ride isn't enough to cover all those years I kept you away from her. Give it time. She isn't going anywhere."

He nodded and took another bite of spaghetti. His time with Reese was good, but how much time would he get with her mother? He was reliving that summer all over again. Only then he thought he had the summer to convince her to stay. This time, he only had until she got a ride out of town.

They continued their meal in silence, and he took their plates and set them aside once they were done.

"Are you sure you don't want to sleep in the house? You can sleep in my bed."

Her brows lifted, and she smiled. "What would your kids say?"

He wouldn't tell her what Basil had already said. "I meant you could sleep in the bed, and I'd take the couch. I don't like you out here in the barn."

"Are you saying it's not safe here?"

He cupped her cheek. "No, it's safe. All I'm saying is you should be inside the house where it's comfortable. I can sleep out on the cot if it makes you feel better."

She covered his hand with hers. "You were always chivalrous, but I need to be here. If Hellion goes downhill, I don't want him to suffer."

They had already discussed what would happen if things went south quickly, and he gave her permission to put him down. It would break his heart, but he wanted what was best for Hellion.

"Okay. You know where to find me. I'm a light sleeper."

"Good to know."

He rose and picked up the tray. "Have a good night, Sara." He hated to leave her here, but she wouldn't budge. In a lot of ways, she was like Carol. He definitely had a type. His women were strong and stubborn.

He entered the house five minutes later. The kids were still at the table eating, but they stopped and stared at him.

"Did you kiss her goodnight?" Lily asked.

"Young lady, would you like to meet my belt?"

She squeaked and shook her head. "No, thank you."

Basil moved his hand through the air like a plane before he made a crash and burn sound. "Your game needs work. Let me know if you need some pointers."

Lloyd held up four fingers. "Don't be late. I think the south pasture needs fence repair."

Basil groaned.

"You want to make that three?"

"I'm not saying a word."

"I knew my smart boy was living in that brain somewhere." He lifted his hand in the air and waved to the kids. "I'm heading to bed. You all exhaust me."

He showered and climbed into bed, and for the next hour, he read a Jack Reacher novel, but his mind wasn't on the book. It was on Sara and what he could do to get her to stay.

Many hours later, he woke to a blood-curdling scream coming from the barn.

CHAPTER EIGHTEEN

She stood on top of the medical kit with her phone's flashlight on, searching the area for the culprit. Something touched her and it wasn't human.

"What the hell is going on here?" The barn door opened and in walked a half-naked man. Not just any man, but Lloyd, who was tugging on his shirt when he got to her. It was a shame he'd found the armholes so easily, because with her eyes on him, she'd almost forgotten about the critter who'd scurried up her pant leg in the middle of the night.

"I'm sorry I woke you. I had an intruder who tried to get in my knickers in the middle of the night."

He knuckled his eyes and swallowed hard a few times before returning her gaze. "Say again?"

She moved the light of her phone around the barn floor again before stepping off the medical kit and walking to the tack room to turn on the lights. "I think I had a mouse in my pants." The tack room lights came on immediately and she flipped the switch to the barn lights, which hummed to life. They were those slow-out-of-the-gate lights that took a few minutes to warm up, but once they did, they provided the light of the sun.

He ran his hand through his hair, but it didn't calm the just-got-out-of-bed look. "On purpose?"

She shoved her phone inside her pants pocket and walked to where he stood. "I'm sure he had a plan, but I didn't invite him."

Lloyd narrowed his eyes. "Why did you assume it's a he?"

She threw her hands in the air. "It could have been a she, but in my experience, anything trying to get into my pants has been male."

He rubbed his face with his palm, and she could hear his calloused hand come into contact with the scruff on his chin. It had that sandpapery sound. What would that feel like against the soft skin of her neck?

"You have a lot of experience with that?"

She was embarrassed to say she did not. "No, can we just forget about my lack of experience and find what snuck into my bed?"

He walked to the cot and reached for the sleeping bag. "My guess is a mouse. Are you afraid of them?"

"I'm not a fan of them. They carry diseases."

"So do squirrels." He looked toward Hellion. "And long-time riding partners." He picked up the sleeping bag and shook it and out fell a small brown field mouse who took off running until it was out of sight. "There's your culprit. He's harmless."

"Until I get the Hantavirus and die."

He reached for her and pulled her into his arms. "You're okay."

She lay her cheek against the soft cotton of his T-shirt and inhaled the scent of him. Everyone had their unique pheromones and Lloyd's had always called to her. Even back then, this was her favorite place—in his arms with her face pressed to his chest.

"You smell the same."

"You remember what I smelled like?"

She nodded. She remembered everything about him. "It's not like I could pick out your soap from the grocery store aisle, but the minute

I smell it, I know it's you. That's how Gordon ended up dating me. He reminded me of you."

Lloyd held her shoulders and stepped back. "Gordon smelled like me?"

She moved into him again and this time wrapped her arms around him so he couldn't step away. She'd had a traumatic morning and needed the comfort of being close to him.

"No, something about him triggered a memory, and that's how we ended up on our first few dates, but he wasn't you. Hell, I'm sure you're not the you I remember, although you're pretty darn close." She squeezed him tightly, afraid that he'd break their contact. How was it one of best nights of her life started with a sick horse, a randy rodent, and a hug from an old lover?

"I'm exactly the same."

She shook her head. "No, neither of us are. Life hasn't been kind and those experiences mold us into who we are. Back then, you weren't a widower with six kids and the pressures of running a profitable ranch on your own." One of his hands rubbed up and down her spine, sending goosebumps across her skin.

"No, I was a young man in love with a beautiful sixteen-year-old. She owned every bit of me."

"Really?" A shiver raced through her.

"You're cold." He led her to the cot. "Have a lie-down."

"I don't want you to leave me. What if another mouse comes?"

He shook his head and chuckled. "You can take care of a gunshot victim but cower from a mouse?"

She sat on the cot and stared up at him. "Not just any mouse. That little guy ... or gal ... had something sinister in mind."

He shook the sleeping bag again and set it at the end of the cot. "No one is doing anything sinister to you on my watch." He lay down on the cot and pulled her to his side before covering them both with the sleeping bag. "We've got a few hours left to sleep." He kissed the top of her head. "It's nice to have you back, Sara."

She didn't care that all the lights were on in the barn. It didn't matter that there may be more mice in her future. All that mattered right now was she was with Lloyd, in his arms, and she was happy to be there.

SHE WOKE to a gasp and a giggle. The giggle was from Lloyd's girls and the gasp was from him.

He rose to his feet and pointed to the door. "Out."

Rose ignored him and walked forward with a tray that held two coffees. "Thought you could use this."

Sara was mortified to be caught in a compromising position. Then again, what was compromised? They were both fully clothed. Even if they weren't, it's not like they could claim they had never slept together because there was evidence in the form of Reese.

"Thank you, Rose." Did she owe them an explanation? She was like a kid who got caught sneaking inside the house after curfew. "There was a mouse."

Rose gave her a confused look. "And you're afraid of them? I thought you were a veterinarian. I imagine you'd be used to the little critters."

Lloyd picked up a cup of coffee and looked at her. "Just cut your losses now and don't say a word. Rose won't let it go until you do. I swear she should have been a lawyer."

Sara took the coffee from the tray and sipped it while staring at Lloyd's kids, who smiled goofily at her.

"Don't you have chores to do?" Lloyd pointed at Basil. "Weren't you supposed to be mucking stalls at four this morning?"

"I was working while you were in here sleeping." He smiled. "You were sleeping, right?"

Lloyd didn't look at all pleased with his kids' teasing. He turned to her. "How about you and I grab some breakfast in town?"

She didn't want to leave the horse, but she was keen on getting out from under the scrutiny of all those Dawson eyes. "Let me check on Hellion. Is there someone who can stay with him while we're gone?"

Lloyd stared at his kids, and they all took a step backward. "They'll take turns. Rose first and down the line. That's an hour a piece."

"You need five hours for breakfast?" Daisy asked.

"You'll pull two hours." He wrapped his arm around Sara's shoulder and led her into the pen where Hellion stood eating his hay. "I'd get moving before I put you all on two-hour shifts."

The kids scurried away like the mouse had that morning.

Sara walked around Hellion, who wasn't nearly as stiff as he'd appeared the day before. When she looked into his eyes, she could almost see his gratitude. Or maybe it was that his third lid was no longer showing, and that was a good sign.

"I don't want to jinx anything, but he's looking better."

Lloyd touched the horse's neck. "You're a Dawson and made of tough stuff."

"He's not out of the woods yet, but I'd say he's turning the corner to good." She wrapped her arms around Lloyd's waist and hugged him. "I'm glad I could be here for him."

He turned to face her. "You were here for me, and that means a lot."

She smiled. "I wasn't your first choice."

He kissed the top of her head. "You were the only choice. I just didn't know it at the time." He walked away from her and filled the horse's hay net and water. "Do you feel safe enough to leave him with a sitter?"

She couldn't help but laugh. "It's like we're talking about our kid."

He walked with her to the door. "He is my kid. I've had him a long time. Now that you're here, he's yours too. Someday, I hope to take a ride with you on his back."

She let her hand find his and they headed to his truck. "It will be a while before he's ready for a ride, but it sounds nice."

"Have you ever ridden?"

"Nope. I was always afraid."

"How about we get rid of that fear later? We can go to breakfast and stop by your place for a change of clothes, and then come back and take a ride. I'll show you the lay of the land. Reese enjoyed the ride, and I'm sure I could make it worth your while."

He helped her inside the truck and walked around to the driver's side.

As soon as he entered, she asked, "Are you offering incentives?"

She smiled at him, and he nodded. "What will it take to get you on the back of a horse?"

"A lot. Do you have any idea how many horse accidents there are each year?"

"None on my ranch. Let me show you. I'll give you the ride of your life."

She wasn't sure if he understood how sexual that sounded. The heat rose on her cheeks until she was certain the lobes of her ears were aflame. "Do you have any idea how that sounds?"

He reached and held her hand. "I know exactly what I'm saying."

She fanned her face with her free hand. "Can we stop by the beach house first? I need a shower—a cold shower."

"Anything you want, Sara."

"Anything?"

"What do you want?"

She wanted a lot of things. She wanted a whole life do-over, and it sounded like he was offering her exactly that, but was it wise to go backwards? "I'm not sure. I keep wondering where all this is leading."

He drove down the dirt road toward town. "Rather than wonder, let's just let it lead us, and we'll see where it goes."

"But I have a life far from here."

He squeezed her hand. "Do you?"

CHAPTER NINETEEN

He didn't want to discount her life in Tulsa, but all the evidence pointed to a life less than perfect. Then again, whose life was ideal?

He sat on the back patio while she showered and changed her clothes. When she returned, she pointed to her jeans. "I have to recycle since I only brought one pair."

"You're staying again?"

"I can't leave the horse alone."

"He's alone right now."

Her expression went from soft to panicked. "I thought you said the kids would sit with him?"

He lifted from the low chair and went straight toward her. "Yes, the kids will watch him. All I meant was he wasn't with you, but he'll still be okay. The kids will call if anything doesn't look right. We're ten minutes away. Five if I drive like you did in that hailstorm."

"I was in a hurry."

"I know. You were trying to get away from me."

"I was delaying the inevitable with you. But what if Hellion's not okay?"

"You're the professional. You said he was looking better. Would you stay on a cot in a barn for every horse with tetanus?"

"No, but I feel responsible. You were delayed in getting home the day of the hailstorm and that was because of me." She walked into the house and picked up a jacket that was flung over the back of the sofa.

"Nothing about your accident changed Hellion's outcome. He got hurt during the hailstorm. If you recall, I was stuck at the diner, and you were hanging out in a field." He chuckled at his pun.

"You're not funny." A sigh escaped her. "Just humor me and let me stay until I'm sure he's out of the woods." She shrugged on the jacket and headed for the door. "Tetanus rarely turns out well."

"I get that, but you don't know Hellion."

"He'll need to be as tough as his name to survive, and I'm going to stay."

"Deal, but you're sleeping in the house."

"I'm not sleeping in your bed."

"Why not? What's wrong with my bed?"

"It's yours and Carol's. Besides, we aren't at that place in our relationship."

He caught up to her. "At least we agree we're in a relationship."

She pursed her lips until they almost disappeared. "We haven't even had a date."

"And yet, you slept with me last night. No wonder our daughter picked up and moved in with a hitchhiker." He laughed as her jaw went slack. He leaned in and lifted her chin until her lips touched and then he kissed her. It was a quick one that he hoped conveyed the message that he was teasing. Since she didn't punch him when he stepped back, he figured he was safe.

"As for Reese, she's got a mind of her own. Regarding sleeping with you ... that's kind of stretching the truth, don't you think?"

They walked out the door and got back into the truck.

He took her hand in his and kissed it. "Did you or did you not lay on top of my body and fall asleep?" It was probably the best night of sleep he'd had in years. When Carol was alive, he feared she'd die in her sleep, so he never slept soundly. But last night, he was like the dead.

"Okay, I slept with you, but I didn't *sleep* with you."

He laughed so hard he nearly clipped a hedge backing out of the driveway. "That's only because I didn't have wine, cloth napkins, and what was the other thing?"

"Flowers," she said.

He turned onto Main Street and pulled into an empty parking spot. "And I thought you had perfect recall. It's candles, not flowers."

He got out of the truck and opened her door. "I want flowers too."

"Done. Anything else on your demand list?"

"Do you ever wear a tie?"

He opened the door to the diner. "Only to weddings and funerals."

"But not dates?"

They walked inside and took the empty booth at the window. "Never."

"So, if I asked you to wear a suit and tie on our date, you wouldn't?"

"That's like me demanding you wear a dress."

"If it's important to you, I would."

"Is what I wear important to you?"

"No, you in a suit and tie seems the equivalent of dressing a cat in a Superman onesie."

It wasn't a deal breaker with her unless she'd changed significantly. She just wanted to see if he'd do it. "I'd say by that description, you ran into Mrs. Brown and her cat."

"Yes, she was in the clinic."

Maisey rushed over with a pot of coffee and a smile. "Hello, you two. Is this a date?"

Sara smiled. "Maybe."

"Nope," Lloyd said. "I'm missing the prerequisite items."

Maisey poured two cups of coffee and leaned her hip against the edge of the booth. "In my book, a date is two people who want to be someplace together."

Sara reached across the table and held his hand. "Then I guess it's a date."

"If you say so."

Maisey turned to Sara. "What are these prerequisite items he's talking about?"

Sara reached for the sugar and the creamer. "Oh, you know. Must eat with their mouths closed and use utensils instead of their fingers."

"And the list gets bigger," he said.

"What's it going to be, kids?"

He ordered an all-American breakfast with bacon and eggs and hash browns and toast. Sara had the same and a side of pancakes.

"Hungry?"

"Famished."

Maisey wrote their order down and tapped the table with her pen. "She's not a cheap date, but don't you love a woman who eats?"

"I love a woman with a good appetite." Maisey left, and he doctored his coffee. "Let's get back to the sleeping arrangements. I wasn't asking you to sleep with me. I was offering you my bed."

She stared at him for a second, and a sly smile spread across her face. "But what if I wanted to sleep with you?"

There was reckless Sara sitting in front of him, and he couldn't deny he liked her. There was a fire burning inside him and he wasn't sure if it was love or lust, or a combination of both.

She was an articulate woman with a witty sense of humor. She mastered the spin of words like no one else could. Even back then, she used them in such a way that they were sweet and seductive. He wasn't sure she was aware of what she was doing then, but he was certain she knew now.

"Do you want to sleep with me or *sleep* with me? I hear there's a difference."

She held out her hands to convey a length that made him blush. "Big difference."

To catch her off guard he said, "So tell me about Jordan."

"It's Gordon, and you know it." Her hands came closer together, and she smiled. "Nothing to brag about."

"And I thought you didn't kiss and tell."

"You asked, and I think honesty in a relationship is important. You informed me we were in a relationship, and I don't want to mess it up this time."

"That we are. Is the thing with Gordon over? I don't want to swim in another man's pond."

She nearly choked on her coffee. "Is that a metaphor for sex?"

"It was that or plow another man's field but that sounded too sexual, and we aren't there."

"Oh, my goodness." She leaned in and whispered, "Do you want to plow my field?" Maisey walked by just as she said the words. The one thing about Maisey was her hearing was excellent. She was tuned into her customers, and that whisper might as well have been a scream.

"Are you gardening?"

Sara laughed, and he thought about her question. When she said it, it sounded awful, but it also sounded wonderful. He couldn't help but wonder if his memory of their encounters all those years ago became a legend in his mind because she was his first love, or if their chemistry was off the charts.

"Not me," Sara said. "Lloyd was talking about plowing a field."

Maisey looked at them and smiled. "I've known this man for years, and he's not known for plowing fields." She pointed to them. "You two are going to be trouble, aren't you?"

He pointed to Sara. "She's trouble. I'm just minding my business, and she shows up out of nowhere and changes everything."

Maisey refilled their coffees. "If there's this tension just being near each other, you've got something special. Don't let life get away from you." She looked over her shoulder at where Ben was cooking. "That man flipped my eggs, and that's all it took. Never let something special slip away for a second time. You only get so many chances to be happy."

Maisey was right. Happiness wasn't something he could take for granted. The kisses he shared with Sara would lead him to believe they had something extraordinary.

"Order up," Ben said from the window, and Maisey rushed off.

"Maisey has a point. When was the last time you were truly happy?"

CHAPTER TWENTY

While Sara considered his question, Maisey rushed by and dropped off their food. "Eat up, kids. By the energy swirling around you, you'll need sustenance when you hit that garden." She winked and disappeared.

Lloyd's phone rang, and her heart skipped a beat. Was it one of the kids calling to tell him Hellion had taken a turn for the worst?

He looked at her with dread and mouthed the name Rose. "Everything okay, honey?" He nodded and smiled. "Thank you for letting me know. I'll tell Sara." He hung up and smiled. "Hellion's tail has settled, and he's moving around some. She wanted you to know that they are keeping a close eye on him and that we should enjoy a peaceful breakfast together."

She was already rolling her bacon in the pancakes, thinking she'd have to eat on the run, but that wasn't the case.

"That's a relief, and it's unusual. These cases rarely go well, and they almost never turn around so quickly."

He forked a bite of hash browns. "I've got a good vet. I'd expect nothing short of a miracle." He chewed his food. "Miracles have been happening since you showed up."

"It's a miracle I didn't kill anyone on the road."

He reached over and took a bite of her pancake. "The locals know better than to be on the road during a storm like that."

She pulled the plate back and out of his reach. "Hey, that's mine."

"You don't want to share with me, darlin'? You're a selfish one. You kept our daughter to yourself for thirty-two years. The least you can do is share a bite of pancake."

"Those thirty-two years weren't all hearts and flowers. You should be grateful you missed some of them." She moved the plate to the center of the table. "You can have all the pancake you want if it stops you from giving me a hard time about it. I already feel terrible. Each time you bring it up, it's like death from a thousand cuts."

"I'm sorry. We both know how hard it was for both of us so let's agree to drop it and focus on other things. What do you want to talk about?"

She picked up a piece of bacon and found it to be the exact crispness she loved. "How long has it been since you've gardened?"

"Are we talking tilling the ground and waiting for carrots to sprout or women?"

She grinned and lifted her shoulders. "Tell me whatever you want."

"Carol was sick for many years before her death. I'm probably as close to being a virgin again as possible. But I kissed Elsa Buchanan." He tapped his head. "I keep forgetting that she's a Van der Veen now, although, being the independent woman Elsa is, I imagine she didn't give up her last name."

"Smart woman. What's the point? You only have a 50/50 chance of making it anyway, and the paperwork is a pain in the butt to change it back, I hear."

"How did our daughter end up being such a romantic when you're such a cynic?"

She took another bite of pancake and considered what her

answer should be. It wasn't his fault that he was the one, and she let him get away.

"My track record for love isn't all that stellar. Given Reese's lack of love experience, I just hope she didn't fall in love with Brandon just because he was the first man to pay attention to her."

"Oh, come on." He pushed his empty plate aside. "I'm a man, and we're not known to be observant, but even I can see those two are a perfect match. I think the powers that be made sure Reese was exactly where she needed to be. Their paths crossing was no accident."

She finished her coffee and reached inside her back pocket, where she'd stuck a few bills. When she pulled them out, the sticky note from the bakery came with them and took flight, landing right in front of Lloyd.

She nearly crawled across the table to retrieve it, but he swiped it up.

"What's this?"

"Nothing," she blurted. "Give it back." She reached for it again, but he held it out of her grasp.

"For it being nothing, it seems important to you."

After several attempts to snatch it from him, she gave up and sank into the seat. "It was a silly thing. You've heard of the wishing wall in the bakery, right?"

"I might have heard a thing or two about it."

"Well, I was writing a wish—a wish that was impossible to grant, so I took it off."

He opened the folded note and read it out loud. "I need a cowboy." He shoved her money toward her. "Wish granted darlin'." He took a few bills from his wallet and set them on the table. "Is your place going to be vacant for a bit?"

She was trying to figure out where he was going with his line of questioning. "I'm the only one staying there for another week, then there's a vacationer arriving. Frank is using it as an Airbnb to cover the taxes and upkeep."

"But no one is expected for the next hour?"

Suddenly, she knew exactly what was on his mind. Was she ready? "You should know the wish was for a car, but Katie told me I couldn't wish for something that was impossible to get, so I needed another C word, and she came up with cowboy."

"Did you put it on the wall?"

"I told you I did."

"Then it's a wish, and you can't take it back."

He slid from the booth and offered his hand. She took it and followed him toward the door.

"Where are you two off to in such a hurry?" Maisey asked.

Lloyd opened the door. "It's time to garden."

Sara turned around and slugged him in the arm. "Don't be telling her that. She'll think you're taking me to your bed."

"Not my bed. You won't sleep in my bed, so we're going to yours."

Before she could reply, he was helping her inside the truck. "I don't want the town to know my business. If you want everyone to think you're easy, fine, but I have standards and morals."

"We walked into the diner together at the crack of dawn and walked out. We have a kid together. Everyone already thinks we're sleeping together." He laughed as he put the truck in reverse and pulled out of his parking place. "Honey, everyone knows we planted a garden before now, so no one cares."

"Is that how you ended up with all those flowers and a spice? You were an avid gardener?"

"You want to talk about the past, or do you want to visit the present?"

He drove toward the beach house, and the closer they got, the more her body vibrated with need. "Is it wise to give in to this desire? I'm going back to Tulsa."

He pulled into the driveway and all but jumped from the truck before rushing to her side. When he opened the door, he continued. "I can't live in the future, Sara. We aren't guaranteed any time but the minute we're in. I can't think about tomorrow, but I promise you

I'll do everything at this moment to make you think twice about going back to Oklahoma. Every second from this point forward, it's my mission to change your mind. You and I know we belong together."

She couldn't argue with him on that front. She didn't date, and the one time she was intimate with another man, it was a disappointment. It was unfair to all men for her to use Lloyd as the benchmark. He was perfect. Not perfect for everyone, but even as a naïve sixteen-year-old, he was perfect for her.

They walked to the door. "Are you ready to claim your cowboy?"

"Katie said it was a done deal, so I guess it's written in the cards."

"Nope, only on your wish, and I'm not ready to give Katie her first failure. Are you?" He leaned in and kissed her. Just as they were pulling apart, her hand went to the knob to open the door, but it swung open and there stood Reese.

"What are you two doing here?"

CHAPTER TWENTY-ONE

Yep, Sara was right. Our daughter was a pain in the keister.

"Why are *you* here?" Sara asked. She turned and looked at him, and if ever there was a woman who looked like a deer caught in the headlights, it was Sara.

"Your mom needed a change of clothes, so we came into town and had breakfast, and now we're getting what she needs." He looked around to make sure they hadn't left evidence that they were already there, but he didn't see anything out of place, not that he would recognize if it were. He wasn't known for paying attention to decorating details.

"Oh." Reese cocked her head like he was speaking turtle, and she was a dove. "I thought someone had been here since it looked like you took a shower."

Sara brushed past her daughter. "You didn't answer the question. Why are you here?" She moved toward the bedroom with him and Reese following close behind.

"Since you were spending time at Dad's, I thought I'd help you by putting in a load of laundry. Also, Uncle Frank called to remind me that he's turning the house over to a renter soon, and since I was here first, I feel responsible for making sure it's a smooth transition. He told me to remind you, so you'd be out on time."

"Who says your mom is leaving Aspen Cove?" he asked.

Reese smiled. "You're staying?"

Sara went into the closet, pulled a few shirts from hangers, and shoved them into a nearby plastic grocery bag before she walked out and tugged open the dresser drawer to get socks and underwear. She tried to hide them from him, but he caught sight of the practical cotton panties before she could shove them inside the bag. They were the kind that got softer with a dozen washings but never sexier. He never understood the obsession with buying lingerie. It cost a ton of money for so little fabric, and its whole purpose was to drive a man wild enough to remove it quickly.

"I'm not staying, but as you know, I'm stuck for now. My options are limited, and I have a patient that requires my attention. For now, I'm here." She looked around the bedroom. "When is the renter coming?"

"Uncle Frank says next week. You can stay with Brandon and me if you want."

Sara brushed a few things that sat on the dresser into the bag, left it there, and walked into the bathroom.

"She'll stay at the ranch," he said.

Sara walked out of the bathroom with her hands filled with beauty products. That was stuff she didn't need either because she was naturally beautiful. With five women in the house, he'd learned to keep his opinion to himself. If a woman said she needed moisturizer that cost twenty dollars when Vaseline cost a couple of bucks, he didn't argue. One of the biggest fights he had with Carol was over skin cream. It was the only time she ever threatened to leave him, and after that, his house had a steady supply of Olay until the day she passed. Come to think of it, his daughters had taken over where Carol left off, and he was sure a good portion of the food budget went to anti-aging skincare routines, but he wasn't stupid enough to touch fire twice and never said a word.

She walked out of the bathroom and stared at both of them. "No one gets to decide where I live and where I'll stay. I'm a grown woman, for goodness' sake, and I'll decide." She picked up the bag from the dresser but couldn't fit another thing in it. Pulling a small suitcase from under the bed, she dumped everything inside, and then went back into the closet to get the rest of her stuff. "What's the point in owning half a beach house if you can't stay here?"

"In all fairness to Uncle Frank, you haven't visited the house in a quarter of a century," Reese said.

She made the same rounds as before and placed the rest of her belongings into the suitcase, closed it, and hefted it into her arms. "Who is this person staying here?"

"I have no idea, but it would seem he wants to make sure it's all perfect. He offered me five hundred dollars to ensure it's stocked and cleaned."

Lloyd loved watching the exchange between mother and daughter. Reese might resemble him, but her hand gestures and mannerisms were all Sara.

"He's paying you five hundred dollars to clean the place?"

Sara smiled. "Easiest money ever since you're like freaking Marie Kondo."

Lloyd had no idea who that was and imagined his confusion was written with exclamation points all over his face. "Who?"

"Oh, she's a professional organizer. One of those house purgers who throws everything away that hasn't been used for a while."

"That seems wasteful. Why would you throw something away that you might need down the road?"

Sara laughed. "Because you probably didn't need it in the first place if you haven't used it."

He took her suitcase and said, "Do you have everything you need?"

Sara twirled slowly in a circle. "If I don't have it, I didn't need it."

Reese walked over and patted him on the shoulder. "You might want to put padlocks on the doors and cabinets, or she'll have you organized in a heartbeat."

"Like mother, like daughter?"

"Don't listen to her. I won't touch anything that you don't want me to. It's not my house."

He tucked her bag under one arm and slung his other arm over her shoulder. "If you feel the need to organize, just let me know. That old tack room could use some love. I've been trying to get the girls to clean it out for years."

"You could threaten them with your shotgun. It seems to get the men in their lives under control," Sara said, and she walked past them, down the hallway, and into the kitchen. She pointed to the wine rack. "Are you refilling that too?"

"It's on the list." Reese pulled a few bottles from the rack and looked at the names. "He's got some good stuff here."

"He's an Arden, and we have excellent taste. Bag that up for me, will you? If I can't have the house, then I can have the wine. Tell Frank to send me the bill."

Reese packed the wine. "Should I tell Brandon you'll be over later, or are you shackin' up with Dad?"

Sara took the bag of wine. "I don't shack up. I have more respect for my reputation. I'll be sleeping in the barn with the mice."

"No, she won't. She'll be sleeping in my bed." As soon as the words were out, he wanted to grab them back, but they sat like three-day-old fish in the air.

"I will not be sleeping in your bed. We've discussed this."

He wanted to yank his graying hair and scream. Difficult women were a habit for him. He married one, and she gave birth to five more. Maybe that came with their indomitable spirit. He imagined that if he liked the fire, he had to endure the heat and a few burns from time to time.

"Your mother is right. I misspoke. She won't be sleeping with me because she's an Arden and her reputation is far more important than common sense. I have offered her my bed without me in it, but she won't take it because she thinks it was Carol's bed. That's not true. Carol had to have a special bed, much like the ones you find in a hospital. We hadn't slept together in years. I was trying to be chivalrous, but that's not a prerequisite for modern women."

He walked to the door.

"Geez, Mom, what's wrong with you? No one would blink an eye if you two got jiggy with it again. Sex is a great stress reducer. It might even make you likable."

He wanted to laugh, but it wasn't the time. He'd have a good one when he was alone. "Jiggy with it?"

"Mom's still living in the nineties, and I try to speak her lingo."

"Young lady," Sara said. "If you want to see nice, stop pushing my mean buttons."

"Uh-oh." Reese walked over and kissed Lloyd on the cheek. "Dad, can I come out tomorrow for a ride?"

He loved that she called him Dad. It took no time for him to adjust to it, and looking at Sara, he was happy she didn't have an issue with it. That was what he was—her father.

"Are you ready?" he asked Sara. "I figure you're itching to get back to your patient. It's not like we had anything else planned."

"Oh my God, you guys were sneaking back here to do it." Reese covered her mouth with her hand. "That's why you were back and surprised to see me. They say kids screw up your love life, but I always thought they meant crying babies or toddlers who refused to sleep alone." She laughed her way to the door. "Who would have thought it was your thirty-two-year-old bouncing baby girl?"

"Where are you off to?"

"I'm going to the pharmacy to get a test. Should I pick you two up a box of condoms?" Reese was laughing so hard she was almost doubled over.

"What test?" Sara asked.

"You know that question you asked me at breakfast? It got me thinking, and I'm late, so..."

Lloyd's head shifted from Sara to Reese. "What are you talking about?"

"Take me back to the ranch, Grandpa."

Lloyd stared at Sara and then looked at Reese. "Are you?"

Reese shrugged. "It's a possibility. Look at that. You might get a two for one. A daughter and a grandchild."

"Me, Brandon, and my shotgun need to have a conversation soon. He will marry you, right?"

"I'm not sure I want to get married."

"Oh, you're getting married," he said.

Reese kissed her mother on the cheek. "Was he always that bossy?"

Sara shut the door behind them and locked it. "I can't honestly remember, but he's right. Brandon needs to step up and do the right thing if you're pregnant. I don't want you to be like me."

Reese rolled her eyes. "Too late. Can't you see? I'm exactly like you, or I was until I met him. I was alone and miserable. I've learned a lot from you over the years, Mom. Now learn from me. There's a fairytale waiting to happen for everyone. You just need to let Prince Charming in. When he rides up on his steed looking for you, hopping on the horse is okay."

They went their separate ways at the driveway, with Reese going to the pharmacy and him taking Sara back to the ranch.

Once they were on the way, he asked, "Do you believe in fairytales?"

CHAPTER TWENTY-TWO

"Fairytales? No. I'm a realist. I know that happily ever after only happens in books. You never read about the bills due, the sick kids, or the cheating spouses. That's real life. In all my years, no one has ridden up on a white horse and saved me from myself. In this day and age, we have to be our own heroes. I taught her better, but she's a romantic at heart."

Her mind reeled from all that transpired over the last hour or so. She almost gave in to her baser needs and slept with Lloyd. What in God's name was she thinking? A kiss here and there was okay. It was a nice distraction, but getting jiggy with Lloyd, as Reese put it, would have been a disaster. She'd been trying hard her entire life to get over him and letting him into her body was the equivalent of letting him into her heart. Nothing good would come of that.

"What are you thinking about?"

"You want a list? Our daughter might be pregnant. I never wanted her to follow in my footsteps. While I don't believe a woman needs a husband to complete her life, I don't want her to wind up single and pregnant."

"That boy will marry her."

She tugged on the seatbelt to give her room and turned toward him. "I'm not forcing her to marry him. That's the wrong thing to do. Even my mother was right about that. She could have marched me straight to the ranch and told your parents I was pregnant."

"And I would have done the right thing and married you."

She had a bitter taste in her mouth because, for the first time, it dawned on her that her mother may have served her well.

"And you would have hated me for taking away your choices."

"I'm not the hating kind, Sara."

She stared at him in disbelief. "Should we ask Poppy and Mark?"

"That's not fair. His father took away all of my options."

She was silent for a moment, hoping his words would soak in. "I would have done the same. I had no business having a baby and would have made an awful wife. I never considered what my mother did as a favor, but in hindsight, she was looking out for me. I had a lot of growing up to do. I was a kid having a kid."

"Your mother did you no favors. She certainly didn't do me any."

"She didn't have you arrested."

He gripped the steering wheel so tightly that his fingers turned white. "I suppose that was a good thing. Can you imagine?"

"No, and I never took the time to because I was angry because she cheated me out of choices. As I sit here thinking, maybe she was doing her best to give me the best life I could have, given the circumstances."

"You don't care if Brandon marries Reese?"

She played out the scenario in her head. One had Reese living her best life without parental interference. She was in her thirties. She didn't need her parents' permission to do anything. The other had Lloyd standing in front of Brandon, shotgun in hand, and Doc with his Bible getting ready to marry them.

"Haven't I meddled enough in my ... I mean our daughter's life? All I want is for her to be happy." Saying that out loud was cathartic. All along, she assumed she knew what was best for Reese, but only the person living their life knows what's best for them. "If she wants to marry and have children and live in Aspen Cove writing romance novels, then I'm okay with it."

Lloyd took in what she said and let the blood drain back into his hands. "I guess I'm old-fashioned. I can't imagine having a child with someone and not marrying them."

"We did it and survived."

"We don't count."

"Of course, we do. Just because you were unaware doesn't make it any less true that we had a child and didn't marry."

"I'm aware of that. I'm not much of a sharer, but I'd be lying if I didn't say that I feel like I've failed you and our daughter."

"Maybe Reese gets her romantic side from you. You sound like a noble suitor in one of her books."

"I've never been accused of being romantic before."

"It's because you haven't paid attention to the women around you. Girls can be tough, and they can do anything a man can, but we have a soft side that needs to be nurtured."

He pulled onto the dirt road and drove under the Big D Ranch sign. "Maybe it's time to Marie Kondo that," he said.

"Probably. A man shouldn't be known only for his big D."

He parked the car. "I'm going to have one big regret today."

She unbuckled her seatbelt and reached for the door handle. "What's that?"

"That I didn't get to remind you of how accurate the ranch's name is." The crimson from his neck continued up his body and settled into a pink in his cheeks. It was funny to see Lloyd blush.

She opened the door. "Reese being home might have been the biggest blessing of all."

"Oh, I don't know. I was thinking the opposite. Our daughter's timing sucks, but now that I think about it, I wasn't there to help or give you the things you needed along the way. You put together a list of must-haves, and I'll endeavor to give you everything you asked for, from wine to cloth napkins to candles."

"Don't forget the flowers."

"How could I when you're constantly reminding me?"

She pointed to the suitcase in the back. "Would you mind putting that in the barn?"

"Yes, I would. I'll put it in my room. That was our agreement. I may not remember a lot, but the Sara I know isn't one to go back on an agreement, and you said you'd stay in the house."

She had no room to argue because she wasn't one to renege on a promise. Her father always said a man was only as good as his word. She imagined a woman was too.

"Fine, but I'll take the couch." She got out of the truck and closed the door. "I'll check on Hellion."

Lloyd picked up her suitcase and walked to the front door. "You'll take the bed."

She walked away grumbling, but her heart was full. She had a beautiful daughter who, despite her, was quite amazing. She was doing what she loved, taking care of animals, and she was surrounded by people who cared about her. Had her life always been that full? If so, she'd never noticed, but being in Aspen Cove brought clarity.

Daisy rose from the cot when Sara arrived.

"How's the patient?"

Daisy walked toward Hellion. "He's been eating and drinking and showing signs of himself. Hellion isn't a patient horse. He's a lot like my father."

"They say animals take on attributes of their owners," Sara said. "Some people start to look like their animals."

Daisy appeared horrified. "Are you serious?"

Sara nodded. "It's true."

"Remind me never to get an ugly dog or cat." She snickered and covered her giggle with her palm. "Won't Mark be surprised when Poppy grows a beard and starts to bleat like her goat?"

"Where is this goat I hear about but never see?"

"Sadie prefers cows to humans."

"I can't say I blame her." Sara inspected the restless horse, and while she'd never seen a horse bounce back from tetanus before,

Hellion was looking good. His muscles were more relaxed, and his eyes had life in them.

Daisy lowered her head. "Can I ask you a question?"

"Anything."

"Do you still love my father?"

It didn't take her but a second to answer. "I don't think I've ever stopped loving your father." That was the truth of it. She could deny it all she wanted, but her heart would call her a liar.

"So that you know, while no one will ever replace our mother, we want our father to be happy, and we'd embrace the opportunity to have a woman's influence in our life."

Sara rushed over to Daisy and hugged her. "Oh, honey, I'm not looking to replace your mother. All I need is a car and a full gas tank, and I'll be out of your hair." A weight like an elephant's foot crushed her heart.

"You're not staying?" A tear slipped from Daisy's cheek.

"Sweetheart, that was never the plan."

"But plans can change, right?"

Plans could change, but hers would not. The Lloyd she knew back then was the same as he was now. He was a man who lived his life with integrity and honor. A man who would do the right thing. While she might have needed a savior three decades ago, she didn't need one now. He was doing the right thing, and she wasn't. She got caught up in the inertia and was following her heart and not her head. That needed to stop. Hadn't her mother beaten it into her all those years ago that logic should always win?

CHAPTER TWENTY-THREE

It had been three days since they'd been caught sneaking into the beach house, and Lloyd was tired of waiting. Was it possible that a part of him was always anticipating her return? Carol knew Sara was his first love, but she was confident enough in their relationship not to be jealous.

"Penny for your thoughts?" Rose was in the stables, grooming Bud.

"I was thinking about your mother, and how strong and confident she was."

"Did she ever meet Sara?"

He nodded. "Once, when she was pregnant with Poppy."

"What did she say?"

That day was imprinted in his memory forever. "She said I had good taste in women."

"That sounds like Mom. Nothing rattled her nerves."

"She was a remarkable woman." He pulled Titan out of his stall and brushed him down. Many people didn't like grooming their horses, but Lloyd found it peaceful. "All you girls are a lot like her. You're made of tough stuff." He checked Titan's shoes. As much as he wanted to trust Basil to look after the horse, he couldn't. His son was still using his boy brains. "How are you girls getting along with Reese?"

"She's awesome. She's taken to riding like a champ. When will you take Sara for a ride? If she's going to stick around, she'll need to learn."

The problem was that Sara wasn't sticking around, which broke his heart. "I don't think she wants to stay in Aspen Cove. She's got a life in Tulsa."

Rose put the brush down and turned to him. "Dad, you're rusty when it comes to wooing a woman."

"Wooing?"

"Yes, a woman like Sara isn't going to uproot her entire life and move to a small town like Aspen Cove unless you give her a reason. Show her everything she has to lose if she leaves."

He hadn't considered that. He'd been kind and accommodating. He'd removed every trace of Carol from his bedroom and gave her his bed while she'd been there. She fought him at every turn, but he wore her down, and she'd been sleeping comfortably while he'd been curled in a ball to fit on the couch.

"What am I not offering her?"

Rose hugged her father. "You, Dad." She stepped back, and being the tallest of his daughters, she looked him straight in the eye. "You need a partner, and she's good for you. You're also good for her. What will it take to get you two to see that?"

"Wine, cloth napkins, and candles." He recited the list from memory. "Oh, and flowers."

"Let me see what I can come up with. There's a storm coming, but it's not supposed to hit until much later. Saddle Bud and Titan and take her to the lower pasture. It's a field of flowers right now, so that's one thing from your list. Let me see what I can come up with for the rest."

It was tempting. "What if she won't go?"

"She'll go." Rose walked toward the door. "I'll be back in fifteen minutes, and I'll keep an eye on Hellion while you're gone. Saddle up, Dad. The rest of your life is waiting."

"And none of you mind that I'm interested in another woman?" They'd told him repeatedly, but he needed to be sure. It was one thing bringing a sister into the mix, but a girlfriend or potential wife?

"Dad, you need a woman in your life. A partner who will give you a reason to get up in the morning. While we love you, your kids aren't going to be here forever. We need to move on too. We want lives and families of our own, and none of us are going anywhere until we know you're okay."

Sara said something about not needing a man to complete a woman. Did he need a woman to complete him? No, but life was better when shared. "I'll saddle the horses and let Sara know we have a date."

Rose smiled. "That's the spirit." She dashed off to the house while he got Bud and Titan ready to ride. Since Hellion wasn't up for the trip yet, he'd been using Basil's horse, and Basil had been driving the ATV.

As he waited for Rose, he considered what she'd said. Show her everything she has to lose. Maybe that was his problem. He'd been showing her what he could offer, but they were things she already had, like a house, job, and family. What she didn't have was him.

Ten minutes later, Rose rushed into the barn with Lily. "We made a picnic lunch for you." They shoved items into the saddlebags of both horses. "Don't mess this up, okay?" Rose said. "She's softened you up, and you're happier. We like what she's brought to your life and think she's a keeper."

He liked her and wanted to keep her too. Not only was she an excellent asset to the ranch, but she was good for him. Because their love had started when they were young, she'd brought back a sense of youthfulness to his life he'd been missing.

"Now go," Lily said. "She's already Marie Kondoed the tack room, and she was eyeing the toolshed for her next project."

He took both horses' reins in his hands and led them outside and down to the barn. When he turned to look over his shoulder, his daughters were waving and smiling. He sure loved all his girls.

He tied the horses to a post and entered the barn to find Sara unwrapping Hellion's bandaged leg.

"Who's a good boy?" She cooed and petted the horse. "Your daddy is going to be so happy. Wait until I tell him you're out of the woods."

"That's excellent news."

Sara slapped her hand over her chest and jumped back a few feet. "You scared the hell out of me."

Hellion nudged at her and nearly knocked her over. "Seems like it jumped into him. He's looking like himself."

"I'm pretty sure he thinks I'm his new mare."

Lloyd walked to his horse and rubbed his neck. "Sorry, man, she's mine. You need to find your own girlfriend."

"I'm yours?"

"I'd like to make you mine. What do you say we take a ride?"

"I don't ride," she said.

Was this how his life was going to be? Would she fight him on everything?

"You do today." He nodded toward the door. "Rose will keep an eye on Hellion. I'll keep an eye on you. Let's go." He didn't wait for her to give in. He took her hand and led her to the horses.

"I'm afraid."

He chuckled. "What kind of vet are you? First rodents and now horses?" While she tried to think of a comeback, he helped her into the saddle. "Bud is a gentle girl and will take care of you. All you need to do is stay in the saddle." He adjusted the stirrups and mounted Titan. "You've been stuck in that barn for over a week. It's time you got to see the ranch."

"But—" Her argument was cut short the minute he moved Titan forward, and Bud followed. She giggled. "I'm riding a horse."

"Yes, you are. You can't be a rancher and not know how to ride."

"I'm not a rancher."

"Not yet, but you're on your way."

They rode for an hour until they came upon a field of sunflowers, and he dismounted.

"What are you doing?" She held on to the horn of the saddle.

"I'm gathering prerequisites for our date." He picked dozens of wild daisies and handed them to her. "For you, my love."

She let go of the horn, clutched the flowers with one hand, and covered her heart with the other. "Are you trying to seduce me?"

The simple answer was yes, but he couldn't be that honest. "I'm wooing you." He mounted Titan, and they continued their walk through the pasture.

"The sky is turning black," she said. "Will we be okay?"

He looked up and didn't like how the clouds looked, but Rose said the storm wouldn't hit for hours, so they should be good. "We'll be fine." Just in case, he turned the horses and headed west toward one of the storm shacks that dotted his land. They'd been put in decades ago in case someone got caught down range in inclement weather. Moments later, a bolt of lightning hit and was followed by a large crack of thunder. "Well, shit. We better hurry."

He spurred Titan into a canter, and Bud followed while Sara bounced in the saddle. He didn't have time to tell her to lift her bottom because the first drops fell, and they were closely followed by pea-sized hail.

"Not again," Sara yelled.

"It's that time of year, I guess." He led them to the shack and quickly dismounted. He helped Sara down and told her to go inside. After unsaddling both horses, he set them free. Their instincts would protect them in the storm. Titan went straight to the lean-to while Bud took off racing toward home.

He carried both saddles into the tiny cabin. For a cowboy, it had everything he'd need. There was a table, two chairs, a camp stove, and a cot. A bookshelf lined the wall, holding canned goods, extra fuel, and a lantern.

"Are you hungry?" he asked.

"Are you crazy? We're stuck in this hellhole, and another hailstorm is coming. Shouldn't we be heading home?"

"Not if you want to survive."

"Didn't you check the weather?"

He hadn't, but Rose had. Was this part of her plan? "I was told on good authority that the storm would come in later."

A loud boom of thunder hit and was followed by the telltale clinks of hail hitting the metal roof.

"Someone lied to you."

"Apparently." He opened the saddlebags and pulled out the bottle of wine first. Next to it was a corkscrew. His girls had thought of everything. "Looks like we have time for a date."

Sara stared at him. "You want a date now? What about the horses?"

"Titan took shelter in the lean-to, and Bud is running for home. I'm sure she's huddling under a tree for now." He pulled out two wineglasses. They were made from plastic but looked real enough. "I've got wine. You've got flowers. See, we're well on our way."

She went to the shelf and looked at the cans there. "It's beans or corned beef hash."

He went to her and brushed her hair back. "Do you think I'd serve you canned goods?" He had no idea what the girls packed, but he hoped it wasn't canned ham sandwiches.

"You did before."

He gently kissed her before guiding her to the table. "You said that wasn't a date. Have some faith." He pulled out two cloth napkins and a battery-operated candle. "Looks like we have everything we need?" He appreciated that his girls were safety conscious. This old shack would go up like tinder if a real candle got out of control. "Candle, wine, napkins, flowers."

"Like I said, do you want beans or hash?"

He tugged three foil-wrapped packages from the saddlebag. Inside one was fried chicken. There was meat and cheese in the next one and fruit in the last container. It wasn't gourmet, but it wasn't

152

canned goods either. He took two plates from the shelf and did his best to make the meal look appetizing.

"Did you plan all this?"

He wished he could take the credit, but he couldn't. "No, I have to tell you. Six kids want us together."

"Seven if you include Reese."

"What about you, Sara? Do you want us together?"

She looked at the cot and then back at him. "My heart says yes. My body says yes. But my head says I'm crazy. In what world do we get to go backward?"

He flipped the switch on the candle and poured them a glass of wine. "It looks like our world is giving us a second chance to get it right. Are you going to take it with me?"

CHAPTER TWENTY-FOUR

As they sipped wine and nibbled on cheese, all she could think about was that cot and how good it would feel to be in Lloyd's arms again. She didn't worry about the hail beating hard on the roof or how it matched the pounding of her heart. She didn't panic over the horses because she knew their instincts would help them survive. She didn't think about how disappointed her mother would be to see that she could take the boy out of Sara's life, but she couldn't remove him from her heart.

Lloyd took his phone from his pocket, found a song, and asked her to dance. She didn't know the song, but as she listened to the words, it was about stripping their lives back to a simpler time. He stared into her eyes, and the life she always wanted was at her fingertips. Cupping her face with his hands, he captured her lips in a toe-curling kiss that made her melt into his arms. That kiss erased all the years they'd lost and almost made her believe in happy endings.

They finally broke apart, and her heart was beating in overdrive. They stayed locked in that moment before subconsciously drifting toward the cot. No words were said as they took off their clothes and climbed under the dusty blanket.

"Are you sure?" he asked.

She wasn't sure about a lot in her life, but there were no second guesses as she stared into her future. "I'm sure."

He kissed her as if his life depended on it. When he rose above her, their eyes met, and he smiled. It wasn't the smile of the rancher but the young man she'd fallen in love with all those years ago.

A feeling of completeness washed over her as he slid inside her. That feeling was immediately followed by panic. She wasn't on birth control.

"What's wrong?" He stopped moving.

"I'm not protected. What was I thinking?"

"You mean birth control?" He laughed. "You're almost fifty. What are the chances?"

He was right. She had a higher chance of winning the lotto. "You're right. Old fears are hard to break. You could say I'm from the camp once burned and twice shy."

He kissed her again, making all thoughts of pregnancy and old mistakes disappear. All that remained was the love that two people had held onto for decades.

When they were finished and lay naked in each other's arms, he turned to her. "I've always loved you, Sara."

She laughed. "Contrary to popular belief, I'm easy to love."

As the storm raged above them, they held each other and discussed a future. He wanted her to stay, and she couldn't help but want to. However, she had her practice to think about and a life in Tulsa. Somehow, they would have to make it work for both of them.

An hour later, the storm had passed, and they were climbing off the cot when the door opened, and Reese walked in. Poor Lloyd grabbed the blanket and held it in front of him without thinking he'd left her naked and exposed.

"Do you have any idea how worried I was? Bud came back alone, and I just knew something bad had happened. But no. You two were in here playing house while I was out searching for you. You didn't answer your phones, you didn't call. How irresponsible could you be?

Sara and Lloyd stood there dumbstruck. The tables were turned. They were the children and their daughter the parent.

"Now." She pointed at their clothes. "Get dressed and get home. You are in serious trouble." Reese turned and walked out the door.

Lloyd dropped the blanket and retrieved his jeans. "Do you think we're grounded?"

"I hope so." When she was a kid, naps and getting grounded were the kiss of death, but as an adult, she was overjoyed at the prospect. They took their time returning to the ranch on the back of Titan. There was too much to see and too many kisses to make up for. As they approached the house, all seven kids were present and grinning.

"She spilled the beans," Sara said as they rode to the stables.

"I think the beans were spilled when the girls packed us the perfect lunch."

He had six kids to worry about. She only had one. Then again, if they were going to make a go of it, she'd have to get used to the fact that she'd gone from being the mother of one to caring for seven. While she knew she'd never replace Carol in Lloyd's children's eyes, she could be something akin to a friend to them all.

Reese marched forward with a stern look on her face. "You took long enough to get here."

"Are we grounded?" Lloyd asked. Though he tried to keep a straight face, he couldn't help but smirk.

"Yes, for a lifetime," Reese said.

"We tried to tell her you'd be fine, but she's a Dawson and hardheaded," Basil said. "And don't blame me for the dent on the ATV. She snagged it as soon as I came in."

Sara looked to Reese, who was rubbing her head. "Hail hurts."

"You went out in that hail? What's wrong with you? You should know better." Hurrying to where her daughter stood, she gave Reese a thorough inspection.

Reese shrugged her off. "I'm fine."

Lloyd stared at the two. "Like mother like daughter." He walked to Reese and looked at Sara. "You can't yell at her for doing exactly what you did."

"Oh, yes, I can. This is a do-what-I-say-and-not-what-I-do moment. She could have killed herself." She crossed her arms and stomped her foot. "You don't get to side with her."

"Oh, yes, I do. She's my daughter, and while she's probably not always right, this time she is." Then he turned to Reese. "I'm also siding with your mother. It was irresponsible to take off in a storm. You could have been hurt badly." He looked at the rest of the kids. "She may be the oldest, but you guys need to have her back. She's your sister. You should have never let her go."

Rose laughed. "Basil tried to stop her, but she tackled him for the keys."

"And won?" Lloyd asked.

"You taught me never to fight with girls. Besides, she had that look of determination. I've seen it before, and I knew I was no match."

Lloyd pointed to the house. "You're all grounded to the kitchen." He pointed at Lily. "Call your boyfriend and tell him to go to Dalton's and pick up pizza for the masses. It's time for another family dinner."

"Can James stay, or is he just the delivery boy?"

Sara watched as Lloyd struggled to let his daughters go. She understood that completely. Letting Reese go was the hardest thing she'd ever done. A lifetime of minutes passed but in reality it was probably only seconds.

"He's close enough to family to count." He turned to Reese. "Call Brandon. He and my shotgun have a date."

Sara laughed. "False alarm."

"You didn't tell him?" Reese asked. "You were supposed to tell him."

"I was distracted," Sara said. "But the tack room is clean."

Basil took Titan and said he'd be in once he'd groomed and fed him.

157

They all headed into the house, and Sara's phone rang. She looked down and frowned because she didn't recognize the number.

"Hello?"

"Can I speak to Sara Arden?"

"Speaking."

"This is Owen's Automotive. You said you'd take the first car I got in. It's a brand-new Jeep. Are you still interested? If so, I can have it delivered tomorrow once the finances are covered."

Her lungs seized, and her breath caught. This was precisely what she wanted weeks ago, but now she wasn't sure. Her heart said to pass, but her head told her not to be crazy. At some point, she'd have to go back. It was inevitable.

"I'll take it." She walked to Lloyd's chair and took a seat so she could give the man on the other end the information he needed. "I'll send the bank draft over immediately."

When she hung up, the only one around was Lloyd. "Are you leaving me?"

CHAPTER TWENTY-FIVE

His gut and heart collided, causing bitter bile to race into his throat. "What happened today that made you want to run?"

She set her phone aside and looked up at him. Her eyes were windows into her soul, and he could see the sadness there.

"I'm not running."

He slumped onto the couch and stared at her. As a logical man and one who heard only one half of a conversation, he owed her the right to explain. After making love to her, and it was love, she owed him an answer. "Are you leaving to head back to Tulsa once the car arrives?"

"Can we talk about this later?"

"No." His voice rose, bringing several girls from the kitchen into the living room.

"What's going on?" Reese asked.

Lloyd scrubbed his palm over his face and rose. "Your mom's new car is being delivered tomorrow. With Hellion on the mend, I imagine she'll be heading back to her life in Tulsa."

"But I thought..."

He knew exactly what she thought. He'd thought the same.

They'd been intimate, which had to mean something. People in love didn't up and leave. His heart was fully engaged, but where was hers? Was she in love with him?

"Mom, what happened to staying?"

Sara shifted uncomfortably in the chair. "That was never the plan. At some point, I must go, but I'll be back." She looked at him. "We both knew going into this, it wouldn't be easy. You have a life here, and I have a life there."

"Bullshit," Reese yelled. "A job isn't a life."

Sara's face reddened, and she balled her fists in her lap. "This isn't some fairytale where your father and I run off into the sunset."

"It could be," Reese said. "Stop being so pragmatic and responsible. Let go of your inner grandma and let your inner teen run the show. How many chances do you think you'll get when it comes to love? One? Ten? One hundred?" She turned to Lloyd. "Do you love my mother?"

He closed his eyes and went back to the moment their bodies connected. It was the first time his heart had been whole in years. The first time everything in his life was right. "I do love your mother." He wanted to shake her and tell her that Reese was right. They wouldn't get another chance at first love, but he didn't want her to stay because he forced her to decide. "But your mom needs to make her own decisions." He walked toward the door. "I'll be on the porch if anyone needs me."

He took a seat and looked at the land before him. This had been his life from the moment he was born. He couldn't imagine another life. Was that how Sara was feeling?

The door opened, and out she walked. "Can I join you?"

"You're always welcome."

She took the seat beside him. "That's the thing. After today, I'm not sure."

He twisted to face her. "Where did you see this going? We didn't talk about what making love would mean to us, but to me, it meant we were together. Was I wrong?"

She leaned forward and put her hands on his thigh. Her touch made his skin tingle. She was the current of life he needed. A lightning storm wasn't the same if there was no lightning, and his life would be less when she left. He'd lived with less over the last few years and wasn't sure he wanted that kind of loneliness to envelope him in the future.

"We are together, but that doesn't mean we have to be together all the time. Tulsa isn't that far away. Why do I have to give up everything to have you?"

The argument was sound. His argument was valid as well. "I never thought I'd love again, and then you entered my life and changed all that. I want what we have, but I want it full time."

"I want what we have too, but I also want what I created for myself. In a world where no one thought I'd succeed, I've managed to raise an amazing daughter and open a thriving practice."

"You told me it thrives whether you're there or not. That means you hired the right people. That alone gives you the freedom to do the things that make your heart happy. Don't I make your heart happy?"

She leaned forward and kissed him. "You make my heart sing, but you're asking a lot. I'm a business owner in Tulsa and to be with you, I'd have to give up that part of me."

He reached up and cupped her cheek. "I'm not asking you to give up who you are, I'm asking you to be with me."

"You're asking me to give up who I am. I'm a veterinarian from Oklahoma."

"I've got a ranch with animals. You can be a veterinarian here."

"There's already one in town. Don't you see that my identity is connected to what I do? That's like me asking you not to be a rancher."

"It's not the same at all. I'm asking you to be who you are in a different place. That's not the same as asking you to be different. If you take a rancher off a ranch, then he's not the same, but if you move a veterinarian from an office to a farm, as long as she has animals to care for, she's still a vet."

When she sighed, her shoulders rolled forward as if the air she'd released had been keeping them propped up. "Can't we try my way for a while and see how it works?"

Was some of Sara better than none of Sara? The logical part of his brain said yes, but the emotional side knew he'd spend a great deal of time pining for her. Each time they parted, it would be like a death until they could resurrect their relationship again. He knew himself well, and that wouldn't work. He couldn't run a ranch full-time when he was empty half the time.

There was no way to get the words past the lump in his throat. He swallowed hard and sucked in a breath of courage. "I'm sorry, Sara, but I'm not willing to settle for some of you when I've had all of you."

She snapped her hands back as if touching him seared her skin. "Are you giving me an ultimatum? It's all or nothing?"

"No. I'm telling you that I can't do part time, some of the time, or when you get the time. I'm a man who needs full-time love. I'm not asking you to choose. I'm choosing for me." He stood, bent over, and kissed the top of her head. "Tell the kids I went to town for a while. I'll be back later." He walked down the steps and climbed into his truck. It was time to buy Doc another beer.

DOC WAS in the bar when he arrived at Bishop's Brewhouse. Goldie was manning the taps. He moved forward slowly until he got to the bar.

"I'll take one and give Doc another," he said. "I'll be buying tonight."

Goldie pulled a frosted mug from the freezer, poured him a beer, and refilled Doc's mug. "Uh-oh. It's got to be bad when you come out of the gate with an offer to buy." She filled up a bowl of bar snacks and set it on the counter before walking away.

"Trouble in paradise?" Doc asked.

"It was paradise a few hours ago, and now I'm troubled." He gulped his beer and set the mug down. "We made love."

Doc held up his hand. "I don't want details."

"I'm not giving you a blow-by-blow account. I'm just saying that we ended up together." He pulled the crumpled napkin out of his pocket. "I've kept this since we spoke last. You were right. All I have is the ranch." He tore the napkin in half and laid the two pieces down. "My kids will always be a part of my life, but they need to have a life of their own." He touched on half of the napkin. "This is the ranch." He pointed to the second half. "After I made love to Sara, this was her, and my life was getting bigger, but she's going back to Tulsa." He wadded up the half representing Sara and tossed it into the trash can behind the bar. "Now I feel like I have less."

Doc stared at him. "Let me get this straight. You made love to the woman, and she left you? I'm no sex therapist, but I can find you one. If things aren't working great between the sheets, I can give you a prescription."

Lloyd held up his hand. "I don't need a little blue pill, Doc." He looked around to make sure no one was listening. All he needed was for a rumor to start about the owner of the Big D ranch not having a working D. "I'm all good in that department. It was good for both of us. Then we got home and ordered pizza, and she got a call that a car was available, and she took it."

Doc rubbed his bushy mustache. "She needs a car, son. Getting a car doesn't mean she's leaving."

"It does. She said she needed to go back to Tulsa. She wanted to do the long-distance thing. For me, it's all or nothing."

"You drew a big line in the sand. Don't forget that her parents drew that line in the sand years ago, and you ended up on the wrong side."

He didn't know how Doc knew the details, but it was a small

town, and nothing was a secret. "I'm trying to end up on the right side this time, but she's determined to go."

"Then let her go."

"That's your advice?"

Doc held up his gnarled hand. "I'm not done yet. Let her go and then show her what's she's missing."

Lloyd picked up his beer and took several gulps. It was the same thing his daughter had told him earlier. He wasn't a romantic, and outside of the candles, flowers, and cloth napkins, he wasn't sure what to do. "I don't have a romantic bone in my body."

Doc grinned. "You don't, but you have a daughter who specializes in romance." Doc picked up his mug and drank it down. "Son, it's not what you know but who you know." He set the empty glass on the bar. "My work here is done. Don't forget, I'm a good tipper, so make sure you leave Goldie something nice." He slid from the stool and shuffled across the bar and out the door.

CHAPTER TWENTY-SIX

Leaving Aspen Cove was the hardest thing she'd ever done, and she'd done it several times. Once when she was a teen, a second time in her twenties, and three weeks ago when her car arrived. The day she packed up and left, Lloyd walked her out and kissed her. Even weeks later, her lips tingled. That kiss alone almost made her stay.

"You're getting flowers every day. What's going on?" her receptionist, Alice, asked. "Did someone die?"

Sara looked at the flowers that were delivered daily, and she had to agree that the vet clinic resembled a florist or a funeral home right before a service.

"No one died. I have a boyfriend." Though Lloyd indicated it was all or nothing, he was still wooing her.

"That guy who keeps calling?" April's eyes bugged out like that was the last possibility on earth. "Is he a normal dude?"

"He's the most normal man I know." Lloyd was a cowboy and rancher. He was a salt of the earth kind of man.

"That doesn't say much since I've never known you to be with anyone." She pointed to the vases sitting around the office. "This isn't normal. You need to do something about your paramour. No one else in Oklahoma can get flowers because he's bought them all."

Never in her life had she received flowers. She wasn't the kind of woman men bought flowers for. That was probably because she had so few men in her life. Alice was right, this wasn't normal, but she liked that he hadn't forgotten her. Every bloom that arrived reminded her of what she was missing. It was probably no mistake that he sent flowers like daisies, roses, lilies, violets, and poppies. One day he sent an herb garden filled with basil. He knew exactly what he was doing, and it was working.

The phone rang, and Alice rolled her eyes. "It's probably him. You should answer it yourself to save time."

She walked over and picked up the phone. "Arden and Baker Vet Clinic, this is Sara. How can I help you?"

"Hello, darlin', did you get the flowers?"

She giggled, took the phone into her office, and sat behind her desk. "You're relentless. Did you take out a second mortgage to pay for them?"

He chuckled. "You can't put a price on love."

"You said you couldn't do long distance. When I left, I imagined you were done with me."

There was a moment of silence, and then he spoke. "It doesn't matter how far away you are, I'll never be done with you. Besides, you're the one who left, baby. It wasn't me."

"How are you?" She loved their daily talks. It gave her a piece of him, but it was never enough. The minute they hung up, she was consumed with emptiness. Each call filled her heart with love, and the end of them hollowed out her soul.

"I've been busy." He cleared his throat. "I wanted you to know there won't be a florist delivery tomorrow. I've got a thing I have to do but know that I'll be with you."

"What thing?" He hadn't told her of any plans. Then again, was she privy to his every move?

"Just something I've got to do." There was a muffled sound, and she swore she heard Reese's voice.

"Is Reese there?" She hadn't talked to her daughter since she left town. It wasn't for lack of trying, but Reese was mad at her for leaving and had gone silent which was worse than when she'd stuttered.

"Nope. She's in town starting a new book. She was here for dinner and talking about a grand gesture. Whatever that is."

Sara knew exactly what that was. "That's when someone in love makes a great sacrifice or a big gesture to prove their love."

"Like if you would have ... if you would have given up living in Oklahoma to move here with me."

That pricked at her heart. Had she made the wrong decision? Deep inside, she knew she had, and right then, she knew exactly what she needed to do. "Are you leaving the ranch?"

"Yep, I'll be gone a day or two. If I can't complete my mission in that time, then it wasn't meant to be."

She figured it had something to do with a cattle auction. Or maybe he was getting Reese a horse. He'd mentioned that a few times in their talks.

"Does it have something to do with a horse?"

He laughed. "You're too smart for your own good."

"You're going to spoil her." She looked at her calendar. How many of her appointments could be rescheduled? If she got in her car tomorrow after her last surgery, she could be in Aspen Cove by the following day.

"I'll do whatever it takes to make my girls happy."

"You're a good man, Lloyd."

"Well, obviously not good enough, but I'm trying."

"I'll miss the flowers and the call."

"Darlin', I've missed you, and I love you." He hung up before she could tell him she loved him back. He'd hear the words firsthand when she walked into the ranch house and told him herself.

She left her office and told April she was leaving the practice.

"You're what?"

She looked at the bags of specialty dog food stacked on one wall and the people with pets sitting on the opposite side of the room. There were two cats and a cocker spaniel who needed shots.

"There aren't any goats or lizards or cats in Superman capes here. There are no hot brownies or pancakes delivered with sass. There isn't a horse named Hellion or a mouse climbing between my sheets. My daughter isn't around to drive me crazy. Most importantly, there isn't Lloyd. I waited thirty-two years for that man and then turned my back when he offered me everything."

April stared at her like she'd lost her mind. "What are you saying?"

"I'm saying that I'm leaving to find my bliss, and his name is Lloyd. I'll talk to Baker, and she can buy me out, or you guys can hire another veterinarian."

April smiled. "I'll clear your schedule."

It should have hurt her feelings that they wouldn't be sad to see her go, but she hadn't shown them her best self either. She hadn't known her best self until she was back with Lloyd. He brought everything good about her to the surface.

At the end of business that day, she told Dr. Baker the plan to relocate to Aspen Cove, and they settled on an agreement to sell her half of the clinic. After tomorrow's surgeries, she'd be a free woman. She considered calling Lloyd to tell him she'd made her choice, and it was him, but wouldn't a surprise be better?

CHAPTER TWENTY-SEVEN

Never in his life had he done so much to win a woman's heart. He'd parked a couple of blocks down from her clinic and took Hellion out of his trailer. He wasn't a white steed, but he was the biggest reason Sara ended up back in his life, and he couldn't imagine doing this without his horse.

"Okay, boy. Let's see if this grand gesture thing works." He'd been talking to Reese ever since Sara left the ranch. She was convinced that all her mother needed was to feel loved. Sara had never been romanced or courted, and since he wasn't there in Tulsa to do that, he sent flowers and called.

Once outside the door of the clinic, he checked the saddlebags for the extras he brought to convince her to choose him and the ranch. He called the clinic number.

"Baker Vet Clinic, this is April. How can I help you?"

The last time he called, it was Arden and Baker, but he let the confusion go. He was here on a mission and straightening out the front desk person was not part of his plan. "Hello. Can you send Dr. Arden outside to see a patient?" He sat tall on his horse and gripped the flowers he'd purchased in his hand.

"No, I cannot. Are you the patient?"

"No, I have her patient outside."

The girl huffed. "Well, bring your pet inside. Dr. Baker can see you."

"I don't want to see Dr. Baker. I'm here to see Sara."

There was a moment of silence. "Is this the flower dude?"

Grand gestures were frustrating. "This is Lloyd, and I demand that Sara Arden come out right now, or my horse will be unhappy."

"Did you say horse?"

He'd drawn the attention of a passerby who stopped and stared. "Can you please send Sara Arden out?" The pygmy goat and potbellied pig he'd placed in the saddlebags were getting impatient.

The door opened, and he smiled, hoping he was displaying a look of chivalry and love rather than annoyance, but when a blue-haired girl wearing black pants and a white smock showed up, his patience stretched as thin as the little goat who stuck his head outside the leather bag and bleated.

"Is that a goat?" the girl asked.

"Where's Sara?"

Craning her neck, she looked up the street. "She left five minutes ago. But she said she had to stop for gas." She looked at him and pointed north. "Sara's a creature of habit." Then she shook her head. "At least she used to be until she quit her job yesterday and said she was going home to you."

His heart swelled larger than his chest could take. "She quit?"

"It must have been all those flowers." She whistled. "Just wait until she sees the goat."

He smiled. "I've got a pig too." He pointed to the other pouch, which started to whine.

The girl laughed. "I need to find me a rancher. You got any with giraffes or gazelles?"

"You said she was a creature of habit. What gas station does she go to?"

"There's one on the corner two blocks up."

He gave Hellion a nudge, and the goat ducked back into the saddlebag. As he approached the gas station, her black Jeep pulled out. He didn't want to push Hellion, but he wasn't letting Sara get away from him this time. The horse sensed his urgency and picked up his pace until he was at a flat-out run down the street. He caught up with her at a stoplight, walked Hellion to the driver's side, and tapped the window with his boot. When she looked up, her expression was priceless. It was one of pure surprise, and when it sunk in that he was there, she was all smiles and tears. The light turned green, but they stayed there staring at each other as car horns blared and people yelled for them to move out of the way.

She pointed to the nearby grocery store parking lot and pulled in there to wait for him.

She was out of her car and running in his direction before he could dismount.

"What are you doing here?"

"I told you I had a thing to do." He slid from Hellion's back, and a whoosh left his lungs when she threw herself at him.

"You said it had to do with a horse." She reached over and patted Hellion. "Weren't you buying Reese a horse?"

He handed her the flowers. "No, I had a delivery to make. I bought Reese a horse last week. I got a two for one. She named hers Fabio. I named the other Juniper."

Tears flooded from her eyes. "You bought me a horse?" She stared into his eyes, and he hoped she could see his love looking back. "But what if I didn't come back?"

He shrugged. "I didn't want to consider that a possibility."

She wiped her tears and looked past him to Hellion. "You're like a knight in shining armor."

A bleat came from one pocket while a grunt came from the other. "I come bearing gifts I hope will persuade you to come back."

She cupped his cheeks and pulled him down to her. "But I already decided I was coming back. I sold my practice, and I was on

171

my way to you. I love you, Lloyd, and I can't bear another day without you."

If his heart was full before, it was near bursting now. "You're coming home to me for good?"

"Yes, you silly man. It's where I belong."

Hellion let out a blustery sound, and Lloyd laughed. "He's been patient enough." He went to the saddlebags and pulled out a gray pygmy goat and a tiny pink miniature pig. "Most men would offer you diamonds, but I'm not sure you're the diamond kind of girl."

She looked at the animals in his hands. "I like diamonds, but these guys are priceless." He offered her the animals, and she cradled them against her chest. "You got me a goat and a pig? You once said they were worthless."

He wrapped his arms around her and held all three of them. "Not if they put a smile on your face." He kissed her slowly, ensuring every bit of his love was poured into every cell of her body. "Shall we go home?"

CHAPTER TWENTY-EIGHT

He'd been down range when he got a text from Sara telling him his presence was required. That either meant she wanted to make love, or dinner was ready. Since it wasn't quite suppertime, he knew what this summoning was about. Sara was making up for lost time, and he was all about pleasing her.

When he got home, he found three of his seven kids taking care of their horses in the stables. "What's up? Why are you quitting early?" It was too early to call it a day. Had they gotten a text too?

"We've been called to a family meeting by Sara," Lily said.

"Is that right?" If the kids were asked to come to the house, then he wasn't getting lucky. "I guess we better hurry."

Lily led Pad into her stall. "What do you think this is about?"

Basil groaned. "I hope we don't have to eat quinoa again."

Since Sara's arrival, she'd insisted everyone broaden their culinary experiences beyond chicken and pizza. She'd been adding various fruits, vegetables, and grains to their diet. Who knew what tonight would hold.

"I don't think it's about food." Lily had a concerned look on her face. "I think she's sick."

His gut twisted. Had he missed something? "What do you mean she's sick?"

She looked at him and then lowered her head. "I came home this afternoon for a lady issue, and she was throwing up."

He hurried through Hellion's care and rushed to the house. Was the universe cruel enough to give him happiness only to take it away? As he hit the steps, Brandon and Reese drove up, followed by Poppy and Mark. That sick feeling in his gut got worse.

"What's going on?" he asked.

Reese shrugged. "I don't know, but I've got some news."

Lloyd pointed to the door. "If your mom called all of us, it's got to be important." His knees nearly collapsed beneath him, and his heart pounded so hard it ached.

They walked inside to find Sara at the kitchen table. Everyone gathered around and took a seat.

She heaved a sigh and looked at each one of them. Her eyes landed on him last. "I called you here because we're a family, and I have family news that will change everything."

Lloyd took her hand. "Honey, no matter what happens, we are here to support you. You're right. We are a family, and family sticks together."

She smiled and nodded. "That's good to hear because this is a big deal."

Reese stood. "Mom, just tell us what's wrong."

Sara grinned. "Wrong? Nothing is wrong." She reached into her back pocket, pulled out a piece of plastic, and set it in front of him.

He leaned down to see two distinctive lines and the word pregnant. He rose from his seat and walked over to Brandon. "Son, I expect you to do the right thing. You will marry my daughter."

Brandon turned white and stared at Reese. "Are you pregnant?"

She gasped. "No, it was a false alarm. I'm not pregnant."

Lloyd went back to where the test sat on the table. "Okay, which one of you is pregnant? Someone is getting married."

All eyes went to Sara, and it dawned on him. "Oh my God.

You're pregnant?" He dropped to his knees in front of her and touched her stomach. "How did that happen?"

She laughed. "The usual way. It turns out I'm not too old for love or babies."

Brandon tapped the table to get his attention. "Sir, what are your intentions regarding my future mother-in-law?"

Lloyd stood and staggered back. At over fifty he never expected to be in this position. If he'd known she was pregnant back then, he would have made her his bride that day. Thirty-two years had passed, but he was the same man and this woman, who he loved, was having his child. "I'll marry her, if she'll have me."

Sara laughed. "I don't need to get married to love you."

"No, but if you love me, you'll marry me." He dropped to his knee and took her hand. "Sara Arden, you stole my heart years ago. I loved you then, and I love you now. The universe has given us a second chance. Will you marry me?"

She cupped his cheek. "I will." She placed her free hand on her stomach. "Are you okay with this?"

"I've got you and my family here. What more could I want?"

"Nothing." She looked at the family. "I know you might have questions or concerns. Does anyone have anything to say?"

"Yes." Basil raised his hand. "Please have a boy."

Lloyd rose and looked at Reese. "When you arrived and said you had news, I prepared myself for news about a marriage or a baby, but I expected it to be about you."

"No, my news isn't quite as life altering, but it is titillating." Reese leaned into the center of the table like she was telling a secret. "I kind of found out who's coming to the beach house."

"I thought the people you prepared for had canceled," Lloyd said. She did all the work to get the property ready, and no one showed up.

"So did I, but apparently, they were delayed. Today, Uncle Frank accidentally sent me an email meant for someone else."

Daisy raised her hands. "Unless it's some hot royal looking for a wife, who cares?"

Reese smiled. "Fine, I won't tell you. I don't know exactly who it is, anyway. All I know is it's someone famous or notorious because whoever is coming requires protection. Vortex Security only protects the rich and famous. I did a little research, and their last twenty clients were movie stars or mafia members.

Find out who's coming to Aspen Cove in One Hundred Dreams...

OTHER BOOKS BY KELLY COLLINS

An Aspen Cove Romance Series

One Hundred Reasons

One Hundred Heartbeats

One Hundred Wishes

One Hundred Promises

One Hundred Excuses

One Hundred Christmas Kisses

One Hundred Lifetimes

One Hundred Ways

One Hundred Goodbyes

One Hundred Secrets

One Hundred Regrets

One Hundred Choices

One Hundred Decisions

One Hundred Glances

One Hundred Lessons

One Hundred Mistakes

One Hundred Nights

One Hundred Whispers

One Hundred Reflections

One Hundred Chances

One Hundred Dreams

GET A FREE BOOK.

Go to www.authorkellycollins.com

ABOUT THE AUTHOR

International bestselling author of more than thirty novels, Kelly Collins writes with the intention of keeping love alive. Always a romantic, she blends real-life events with her vivid imagination to create characters and stories that lovers of contemporary romance, new adult, and romantic suspense will return to again and again.

For More Information
www.authorkellycollins.com
kelly@authorkellycollins.com

CPSIA information can be obtained
at www.ICGtesting.com
Printed in the USA
BVHW050024140223
658395BV00025B/428